FILTHY RICH

JULIE KRISS

Read more about Julie at www.juliekriss.com

ONE

Samantha

THERE ARE three kinds of bosses: the kind you dislike, the kind you hate, and the kind you loathe.

As an executive assistant to CEOs, that was my philosophy— honed by working for the most demanding bosses in New York City. Years of working for rich, entitled men had never changed my mind.

But with this job, for the first time I wondered.

It was six thirty in the morning. I was already up and dressed for the office, standing in my kitchen eating a bowl of oatmeal with berries on it and sipping a coffee. I'd gotten out of bed half an hour before my alarm was supposed to go off. My little Hell's Kitchen apartment was dim and quiet, only the faint traffic sounds of 9th Avenue floating up ten floors to my window. My makeup was done and my hair was up. I reached for my cell phone to look up my to-do list for today at the office.

And as my thumb hovered over my phone screen, I realized that for the first time in nine years, I was thinking about my work day without a sick feeling of anger or dread. In fact, I was almost... looking forward to it.

That couldn't be possible, could it?

I swiped my phone on and opened my schedule app, the one I shared with Aidan Winters, the CEO of Tower Venture Capital. As Aidan's executive assistant, I had access to his schedule and he had access to mine. At a glance, I could see that Aidan's first meeting was at ten o'clock. It was with Rob and Jared Egerton, the brothers who headed up Ghosted, one of New York's hot startups. I had originally booked the meeting to end at eleven, but the app showed me that Aidan himself had extended that to twelve.

I knew what that meant: good news for the Egerton brothers.

Basically, the job of a venture capital firm is to give other businesses money—lots and lots of money—for a return on investment. Tower VC had millions of dollars—tens of millions, maybe. Aidan's job, which he was a genius at, was to take those millions and turn them into millions more.

The Egerton brothers must be looking for venture capital for Ghosted, an app that allowed you to track exactly who has ghosted you on dating sites. It was a silly product that had gotten splashes of media attention when a couple of celebrities admitted to using it. They were about to go public in a few months. They'd gotten a meeting with Aidan, which was a coup in itself. But if Aidan thought the meeting was going to go long, it meant he'd pretty much made up his mind already.

Which meant there was going to be a deal.

After three months working for Aidan, I knew the pattern. Short meetings were a no; medium meetings meant he was undecided. Only twice had I seen Aidan extend one of the meetings in his schedule, and both times had resulted in a deal.

Standing in my kitchen, I smiled to myself. This was what it meant to work for Aidan Winters: I knew the outcome of a potential high-level multimillion-dollar deal hours before the meeting even happened. And he hadn't even had to tell me what he was thinking.

If you think this is the story of a girl who hates her boss, think again.

TWO

Samantha

BAD BOSSES WERE PRETTY MUCH a specialty of mine.

It ran in the family. My sister, Emma, older and bossier than me, ran Executive Ranks, a company that specialized in providing executive assistants to the most high-level clients. Emma recruited executive assistants, trained them, tested them, and ran extensive background checks. Most of the potentials she took on never made the final cut. The few who went the distance were personally referred by Executive Ranks and placed in highly paid, highly confidential positions.

I had been her first, and best, recruit. For nine years, I'd worked for every kind of bad boss there was: raging assholes, doddering old fogies, entitled jerks who'd inherited multimillion-dollar businesses from Daddy. I'd worked for alcoholics and gropers and men who couldn't recall their own children's names. I'd been called *sweetheart* and *little girl* and every foul name in the book. I'd picked up dry cleaning in a snowstorm and driven to New Jersey to deliver a Christmas gift to a mistress while my boss was at home with his wife and kids. Working for some of New York's richest, most powerful men was high-stress work and it wasn't fun, but it paid well.

And I was good at it. The best, in fact. At twenty-nine I was the most sought-after executive assistant at Executive Ranks, with the highest pay grade. After the last CEO I worked for retired, I was available only to the highest, most vetted bidder.

That turned out to be Aidan Winters. He was thirty-four, brilliant, mysterious, and apparently filthy rich.

He was also gorgeous and single. But that was none of my business.

I stepped out of the hired car in front of the Tower VC offices and thanked the driver. That was one of the perks of working for Aidan: he had a car and driver take me to work and home every day. He'd had to add it to his offer to Executive Ranks in order to sweeten the deal and hire me. It worked.

The Tower VC offices weren't on Madison Avenue or Wall Street; they were in Tribeca, a smaller, funkier area of New York. Tower only had twenty employees, so there was no need for a grand suite of offices or a building with a name on the side. Just the top floor of a renovated, century-old building with open, high-ceilinged lofts. The building was modest and the interior design was understated, but none of it was cheap. Tribeca real estate was expensive, just like any real estate in New York City.

I shouldered my purse and huddled in to my knee-length trench coat. It was early May, and the weather could go in any direction, from stifling warm to freezing cold. Today was sunny, but the wind was cool, reminding everyone that spring wasn't fully happening yet.

Inside the front doors, I greeted the security guard, swiped my pass, and got in the elevator, a beautiful retro cage-like contraption that had old-fashioned doors. When they'd renovated this building, they'd redone the elevator so the workings were safe and modern but the appearance was still vintage 1950s.

When the doors opened on the seventh floor, I was greeted with the smell of coffee. It was eight o'clock, thirty minutes before Aidan was due to arrive. A good executive assistant always gets to work before her boss does, so that he never walks in to a delay or a problem.

I walked to my office—Aidan and I had two of the only enclosed offices in the huge space—and put down my purse and my coat. I walked back out to the coffee station to get myself a cup. There was no crappy gasoline-grade coffee at Tower—only the best, and it was unlimited for employees. It was generous, but Aidan had once told me that since he'd put in the coffee station, productivity had gone up. "People do more work," he said, "when they aren't doing constant Starbucks runs. Don't tell anyone I said that."

Next to the coffee station, I could see three employees huddled around a laptop.

"Wow," said Lianne, one of our accountants. "So that's what he was doing last night."

"Solo or with a plus-one?" Jason, one of our HR people, leaned in, trying not to tip his coffee cup.

"Definitely solo." Tara, the office manager, clicked on a photo, and she and Lianne sighed. "God, he's hot as ever." She glanced up at me. "Hey, Samantha. Have you seen where our fearless leader was last night?"

I came closer and looked at the screen. It was a New York gossip site. The photo was of Aidan Winters, wearing a black suit and black shirt. He was ascending the steps of a swanky hotel, his head tilted slightly toward the camera as if he'd just noticed the photographer. His dark hair was combed back, his jaw clean-shaven. His hand was resting lightly on one lapel, as if he were in the process of smoothing it, and an expensive wristwatch gleamed from his cuff. His high cheekbones and perfect mouth were hard and his dark eyes were a little cold, as if glimpsing the photographer had annoyed him.

The headline read: *Who will land the Man in Black? Winters arrives alone at yet another event. No one has caught New York's richest—and hottest—bachelor yet!*

The Man in Black. One of the gossip sites had started using that, and the name had caught on. It wasn't a bad nickname, because Aidan really did wear black—he didn't wear any other color. Even when he wore a suit, his shirt and his tie were always black. It made him look calm and a little bit sinister, like he didn't care what anyone thought about what he wore. It unsettled people. I sometimes wondered if that was the effect he was going for.

The other thing the gossip sites loved about him was his looks. There was no denying that Aidan Winters, with his dark hair, perfect jaw, dark eyes, and perfect body beneath the black suit, was a gorgeous man. He was also single, and unlike most other rich bachelors, he wasn't seen with a lineup of different women. Whenever he attended public events, like this one, he attended alone.

I sighed and sipped my coffee, my gaze lingering on the photo of Aidan on the hotel steps. "They really don't want to leave him alone, do they?"

"Why would they?" Lianne said. "Single, gorgeous, rich, brilliant. He has it all."

"Don't forget mysterious," Tara said.

"Definitely. I mean, do you think he can't get a date?" Lianne scrolled down. "That's insane. Even if he wasn't into women, he'd still have any date he wanted. Why does he go to every event on his own?"

There was a pause as the three of them looked at me.

"What?" I said. "I know as much as you do."

"You must know *something*," Lianne said. "You know all the inside secrets."

"Is there a secret girlfriend?" Jason turned toward me, leaning in. "You can tell us."

"No, no," Tara said. "He had his heart broken years ago, and he can never love again." She put her hand on her heart. "He just needs the love of a good woman to heal him."

"Forget it," Lianne said. "He's Christian Grey. The secret room with the whips and chains and whatnot. *Not* that I read that book, mind you."

They laughed, but my gaze moved back to the photo. There was something about the perfection of him, the carelessness of the angle, that drew me in. His hand on his lapel—it was a capable, masculine hand, flawlessly formed. I'd seen Aidan's hands every day, but I stared at the hand in that photograph. Then I looked at his icy eyes. I wasn't lying to the others—I had no idea who Aidan dated, if anyone, or when.

He must get dozens of potential offers—so he must make the decision to attend events alone. Why?

None of your business, Samantha.

I shook myself out of my trance and held up my hand. "Oh, my God. Enough, you guys. The event he was at last night wasn't in his schedule. He must have decided to go on impulse." I pointed at the computer screen. "Now, get rid of that before he gets here. And don't let him hear you talk like that. He doesn't care about gossip, but hearing his employees repeat it annoys him."

They groaned good-naturedly, but Lianne closed the webpage and they went back to work. Aidan wasn't a boss who had tantrums or screaming matches. No, he got *annoyed*. That was all. And that was plenty for anyone with two brain cells to

rub together. If you wanted to keep your j
the good coffee, you didn't annoy Aidan.

I only had ten minutes now before Aı
unlocked his office. It was big, high ceilinged, ι
industrial like the rest of the office. There werℓ
the main room, but there was a bank of floor-to-c   .ows
overlooking the street. From here, Aidan could seℓ ..ie bustle of
Tribeca as he worked in privacy.

I powered on his MacBook, typing in his password. I checked
the surface of his glass-topped desk to make sure nothing was left
there that he didn't want to see. I did a quick sweep of the room
to make sure that housekeeping had emptied the garbage and
wiped down the glass and the polished wood. Aidan was a man
who brought his own coffee, so I was spared that task.

When his office was ready, I locked it again and went back to
my own. My office was much smaller than Aidan's, and it had
windows to the main room—probably so that my boss could keep
tabs on me if he wanted to. I also had a window to the street, though
it was smaller. It was fine with me. I'd worked in ugly cubicles and
cubes that froze with air conditioning. For one memorable assignment, I'd actually shared office space with my boss—never again. At
Tower I had sunlight, a nice desk, and just enough privacy. I liked it.

I logged in to Aidan's email account and began to sort the
emails that had come to him, setting aside the high-priority ones,
filing the low-priority ones separately, and deleting the trash.

The highest-priority items were always from Aidan's partners
at Tower VC. This morning there was a message from Noah
Pearson, the partner in L.A. It was short, as a lot of the partners'
emails were. *We need to meet in Chicago next week*, it said.
Tuesday at the Chicago office. Eight a.m.

I filed that one so that Aidan would see it first. While Aidan
worked here in New York, one of the Tower partners worked in

, there was one in L.A., and a fourth partner worked in as. The company lore was that the partners had all been roommates when they were down-and-out teenagers in Chicago. Now, all these years later, all of them were rich and they were still business partners and still friends. While Tower had spread to several offices, the Chicago office was still home.

In the three months I'd worked for Aidan, the partners hadn't had a meeting like this. I wondered why one was being called now.

I felt a change in the atmosphere, something that made my spine straighten. Maybe it was a scent or a breath of air. I looked up to see Aidan standing in my open doorway.

He was wearing his customary black suit, with black shirt and tie. It fit his long, muscled body, just as all of his suits did. He was leaning casually against the doorframe of my office, a coffee in one hand. He was freshly showered and freshly shaved, and his dark eyes with their dark lashes were watching me with seriousness and a tinge of humor.

"Good morning, Samantha," he said.

I smiled at him over the top of my laptop. It wasn't hard at all to smile at the sight of him. "Good morning, Aidan."

"Email is engrossing?" he asked, sipping his coffee.

"Your email always is."

"I'll take your word for it, since I haven't read it."

Unlike most of the CEOs I'd worked for, Aidan didn't get work emails on his phone. He had a private number given to only a few people, and if one of those people needed to reach him urgently after hours, they could text him. Otherwise, he'd read his work email when he got around to it.

It was part of his mystery. Every CEO I'd worked for had been glued to his texts and emails night and day. Aidan wasn't. What did he do in his off-hours? My only experience was with workaholics, so I had no idea.

Well, I knew what he'd done in his off-hours last night. He'd gone to a gala. Alone.

"Is there a reason Noah Pearson is calling for a partner meeting by email, instead of texting you?" I asked. All of the partners must know that an email would get to Aidan much more slowly than a text to his private line.

Aidan shrugged. "Probably because he knows you'll see an email before I do, which means that whatever he wants will actually get done."

"But he's never met me," I said. I hadn't met any of the partners yet, since they weren't here in New York.

"He doesn't have to meet you," Aidan said. "He knows that I turn up everywhere I'm supposed to, on time and fully dressed. That means you must be competent. If he texted the request to me, I'd never show up."

I shook my head. "Thank you for the compliment, but I doubt that." Aidan was one of the smartest men I'd ever met. "I've never seen you forget anything."

Aidan pushed his shoulder off the doorframe. "I didn't say I'd forget. I said I wouldn't show up. You keep me honest, it seems. Can you meet me in my office for a few minutes?"

"Of course," I said, standing. I grabbed my notebook and pen and followed him back to his office.

When we were alone with the door closed, I felt the familiar rush of quiet excitement I always had. This was new, and probably a bad idea. I'd never felt attraction for any of my bosses before. Some of them had made passes at me, or at least made it known that they were open to the idea of sex. It was creepy, but it was part of the job. Men who were as rich and powerful as the ones I worked for saw sex as just another acquisition, something that came easy to them from anyone they chose.

If I wasn't comfortable working for a particular man, I left.

And if a man wanted to fire me for saying no, that was his problem. I knew my worth, and I wasn't going to starve.

But I'd never worked for a man as good-looking as Aidan. Aside from that, there was a quiet zing of chemistry between us. It made me remember that I was single and not dead from the neck down. It also made me remember that I hadn't had sex in a while. It was difficult not to notice how easily Aidan moved in his expensive suits or how good he smelled. The fact that he was single, with a mysterious reputation as a loner, only made him more attractive.

Still, I was a professional, and this was my job. A high-paying job that I was very, very good at. I could handle a sizzle of attraction without acting on it. I wasn't about to make Aidan feel uncomfortable by fawning over him. If a man couldn't do that to me, then I couldn't do it to him either.

We worked well together. That was what mattered.

Still, as I sat in the chair across from his desk and crossed my legs, I felt that zing again. It made me feel feminine, which I hadn't felt very often lately. I found my gaze lingering on one of Aidan's gorgeous hands, and I pulled it away.

"Is everything ready for the meeting at ten?" he asked me.

Right. *Wake up, Samantha.* "Yes. Coffee is ordered and the room should be set up. I'll go double-check that when I leave here."

"The Egerton brothers," Aidan said with a grim tone to his voice. He ran a hand through his dark hair. "I hate doing the internet startup deals."

"But you're going to do a deal," I said.

"You guessed from the schedule?" He shrugged. "The metrics look good, and the profit potential is there. Though the internet deals are more Dane's area of expertise."

Dane Scotland, the Chicago partner, was the programming wiz. Aidan was the expert in real estate deals.

"Is there anything else on my schedule?" he asked.

I checked my phone. "No. Not that I know of."

Aidan's eyebrows rose. "That you know of?"

"I just mean that last night..." Shit. What an idiot. Why was I bringing up the gala last night? It had just slipped out because it was on my mind, and now I'd dug myself a hole. "Maybe I didn't have your schedule right," I finished lamely.

"You're asking me about the gala last night." Aidan leaned back in his chair.

"Not really." And damn it, now I could feel my cheeks get hot. This never happened to me. "What I mean is, it's none of my business. I'm only concerned in case I missed something I was supposed to know." A lot of my bosses needed my help with attending events: making sure formalwear was acquired and cleaned, ordering drivers, sending gifts.

"And how did you know I attended?" The corner of his mouth quirked, but his gaze was calm. I'd never annoyed Aidan, and I didn't want to start today. Especially after warning the others about it.

"I may have seen a headline somewhere by mistake." He said nothing, so I decided to handle the situation by turning it around. "Honestly, it was an accident. I don't Google you in my off-hours, Aidan. If you think I do, that's your ego talking."

He blinked, and then his expression relaxed. For a second, the Man in Black almost smiled. Then he said, "Fine, Samantha. Let's move on."

THREE

Aidan

SAMANTHA RILEY HAD WORKED for me for three months, and I'd never seen her quite like this. She was... flustered. Actually flustered. By me.

She was right—it was my ego talking. My ego and maybe some wishful thinking. The assistant I'd had before her had been fifty-eight and a grandmother; she was tough and entirely competent, but there was no denying she looked nothing like Samantha. Definitely not.

Samantha was sitting across from me now, her legs crossed, her notebook on her thigh. She wore a dark gray pencil skirt and a light blue blouse. The skirt came exactly to her knee and the blouse covered everything it was supposed to without being dowdy. Her dark blonde—some would say dirty blonde—hair was tied up neatly off her neck. Her makeup was expert and understated, as was her jewelry. She knew exactly how to dress as the professional she was.

Except for the shoes. She was wearing low black heels—with an ankle strap. It was subtle and it was very, very sexy. Every pair of heels she wore to work had that ankle strap—the black ones, the brown ones, the ones with the open toes, the ones with the closed toes. Samantha never wore ultra-high spike heels or flats. She wore low heels, expensive and feminine. And every pair had an ankle strap.

I shouldn't be paying so much attention to my assistant's feet. But fuck it. I was.

Maybe it was so that I wouldn't be tempted to pay too much attention to the rest of her. Samantha was a genuinely beautiful woman, with blue eyes offsetting her blonde hair, a small, straight nose, and her mouth... No, I definitely wasn't looking at her mouth, the lush softness of it, the way the top lip curved just so. Her body was perfect beneath the skirt and blouse: slim waist, sleekly rounded hips, small high breasts cupped neatly in her bra. I didn't look at those either, because when I did, I imagined what they would look like in my hands while she rode me.

I sound like a pig, but they say the average male thinks about sex every seven seconds. I was no exception.

I had control. I never let Samantha know what I was thinking. She was too important, and we worked too well together. She was very fucking good at her job—intelligent, focused, impossible to rile. A good executive assistant is worth her weight in gold, which was pretty much what I paid her. So I kept my thoughts in line, my mouth shut, and my dick down. Besides, in three months she'd never given the slightest hint that I affected her any more than the vase of palm leaves in the front lobby did.

Until now.

It had been brief, but it was there. Her cheeks had flushed and for a second she'd squirmed in her seat like a teenager. Then she was in control again. It was the gala—something about my attending it had set her off. I wondered what.

"It was an impulse, you know," I said.

She blinked at me, back to business now. "I beg your pardon?"

"My going to the gala last night. I'd forgotten I even had the invitation. I decided to go because I was bored."

Bored and restless, dissatisfied. But I didn't tell her that.

"Oh." Samantha smoothed a small lock of hair behind her ear. "I see."

"When I go to these events, it's free publicity for Tower VC. I found the invitation last night, and I was at loose ends. So I went."

She nodded. "Aidan, you don't have to explain yourself to me."

I did, though. Something about the gala was still bothering her—I could see it in her expression. Instead of pressing, I decided to change the subject. I tapped my laptop awake. "So Noah wants a partner meeting?"

"Next Tuesday in Chicago." She sounded relieved to be talking about something else. "I think I can clear off your schedule. Should I make the arrangements?"

"I suppose so." I was surprised Noah wanted to leave the roster of actresses and models he was dating in L.A. to come to Chicago for a meeting. My old friend had slept with half the women in Hollywood; it would have to be important for him to take a break from womanizing. "I'll fly in Monday, and I'll spend an extra day. Book me back on Thursday morning, first class. And book yourself to come with me."

Samantha had been writing in her notebook, but she went still. She looked up at me in surprise. "You want me to come?"

Very much. Shut up, brain. "Yes, I think so," I said. "It's the perfect chance for you to meet all of the partners in person. That is, if you're available to take the trip?"

I was fishing. Samantha didn't wear a wedding ring. I wanted to know if she'd say *I'll check with my boyfriend* or, hell, *I'll check with my girlfriend*. At this point I had no idea. And it was petty, and completely over the line, but I wanted to know.

"I can go," Samantha said right away. "It's no problem at all."

Which didn't mean she was fully single. Maybe she just really wanted to go. She straightened a little in her chair, her eyes quietly sparking with a hint of excitement. Then I remembered something that had been on her CV.

"You're from Chicago, right?" I said.

She nodded. "I haven't been back since I started here."

"All right, then. Consider Wednesday a day off in Chicago to do whatever you want. That's what I'm going to do. See friends, family, that sort of thing." I wasn't looking forward to visiting my mother, but it was unavoidable.

Samantha smiled. I'd never seen her smile like that—a full, open, genuine smile of happiness. "Thank you, Aidan. That's sweet of you."

Sweet. No one ever called me that.

But if it made her smile, I would take it.

FOUR

Aidan

"DANE, I have no idea what the fuck you're talking about."

It was five minutes to ten, and I was on my way to the meeting with the Egerton brothers. I'd sent Dane Scotland, the Chicago partner, the briefing notes and he was trying to tell me how to handle the meeting.

"Just ask them about the API," Dane said, his voice its usual pissed-off growl. "It doesn't look like it's been fully tested. I want to know the plan for that. No API means no integration and no product."

I closed my office door behind me and walked through the open space toward the glassed-in meeting room. The phone to my ear, I glanced around for Samantha and saw her leaving her own office, heading toward the front desk. She gave me a nod and a lifted eyebrow, which meant, *They're here and I'm going to get them. Okay?* I nodded at her and turned back toward the meeting room.

"I can ask them, but the answer will mostly be over my head," I told Dane frankly. "You know how I am with web guys. These internet startups are all based in New York. I don't know why we don't switch offices."

"Because I hate New York," Dane reminded me. "It's a city full of fakers and assholes."

"I live here, you know."

"You're only there because the company sent you there."

"Ava lives here, too." My sister lived in Brooklyn. Since Dane and I had been friends since we were fifteen, he was well acquainted with Ava. "She actually chooses to be here."

"Fine, then," Dane said. "Ava's the exception. Everyone else in New York is an asshole."

I pulled the meeting room door closed behind me. "I'm telling you, Dane, real estate is my expertise. I should be in Chicago while you handle the New York stuff."

"Talk to Noah and see if you can get him to trade with you. It's time he left L.A. I think his dick is going to break if he fucks any more models."

I sighed. Dane's way with words was one of the reasons I hadn't pushed him to come to New York before now. He needed a little polish first. "Noah would be useless in New York, and I'd be useless at the entertainment deals," I said. "And Alex works best in Dallas, doing the oil and ranching deals. No, it has to be you and me trading places."

"You're just sick of New York and want to come back," Dane said.

"I like New York." Through the glass, I could see Samantha leading two men to the meeting room. She was probably what I liked most about New York, but I wasn't about to say that. "You're just stuck in your ways."

"Chicago is home."

"The women are better here."

"That's a fucking lie, and you know it. You're not even dating anyone."

"How the hell do you know about my sex life? No, scratch that. How the hell does *everyone* know about my sex life?"

"I don't know about everyone, but I've known you since we were fifteen. The story is always the same. Women try to get into Aidan's pants, and Aidan says no. Are you telling me it's different in New York?"

Fuck, sometimes it was hard to work with people who knew everything about you. "Piss off, Dane," I said. "I have to take a meeting now. The meeting *you* should be at."

"Like I say, ask about the API. And don't screw it up." He hung up.

I sighed and dropped my phone into my pocket as Samantha opened the meeting room door. "Gentlemen, this is Aidan Winters," she said smoothly. The brothers introduced themselves —Rob was the taller one, Jared was shorter with shaggier hair— and Samantha looked at me. "Do you have everything you need?"

Everything except you in here, sitting next to me and getting me through this damn meeting. "Yes, Samantha, thank you."

"You're welcome," she said politely, leaving and closing the door behind her.

Rob Egerton put his hands in his pockets, his grin exactly matching the shit-eating one on his brother's face. "Samantha, huh?" he said to me. "Is she single or what?"

"Excuse me?" I said.

"She's hot, man. Really fucking hot. I mean, that ass."

Jared Egerton shook his head. "The Man in Black," he said. "No wonder he's a legend. He gets the best pussy in New York."

I looked from one brother to the other, waiting for the shoe to drop for either of them. It didn't.

Seriously. Why was everyone but me so direly fucking stupid?

"That's all you have to say?" I prompted them.

"What?" Jared said. "I'm just saying I'd do her, that's all. No big deal."

"Okay," I said to the Egerton brothers. "We're done."

"YOU KICKED them out just like that?" Noah laughed through my speakerphone. "You've always been ballsy, Aidan."

"That's one word for it," Alex said from Dallas.

Dane said, "What did they say?"

We were on a conference call. I was alone in my penthouse, because I'd been too fucking angry to stay in the office and keep my cool. I was sitting in my home office, my phone on my desk. I had my laptop open and was scanning through reports as we talked. "They were surprised, then they said some shit about me being an oversensitive pussy, and then something about how I would be sorry. I confess I wasn't listening by then. And then I escorted them out."

"Don't mess with the Man in Black," Alex said. "You don't even sound angry."

"Angry?" I raised my gaze from my laptop, thinking. "That's an interesting thought."

Dane groaned. "Oh, no. You're definitely angry. Those guys are fucked."

"I can behave," I told him.

"They're totally fucked," Alex agreed.

"You're a cold, cold bastard," Noah said. It was early in L.A., and I heard him crunching on something, probably cereal. "You have a sliver of ice where your heart is supposed to be."

I frowned, annoyed. "All right, let me ask officially. Does

anyone have a problem with what I did today? An objection to me kicking the Egerton brothers out of the building for referring to my assistant as pussy?"

Silence.

"Speak now or shut up about it forever," I said. "Three, two, one."

"It's fine, Aidan," Dane said. "They were out of line. We don't do business with guys like that."

"Note to self," Noah said. "Do not make a comment about Samantha, good or bad. No matter what. Just stay off the topic entirely."

He was ribbing me, and I was going to argue, but I decided against it. "You know what? You're right. No comments about Samantha. She's off limits. I'm bringing her to Chicago, by the way. None of you even breathe in her direction."

"Jesus, you've never talked about a woman like this," Alex said. "What's going on?"

I rolled my shoulders, feeling how tense they were. "What's going on is that she's brilliant, qualified, and utterly competent. I pay her an exorbitant salary, and I want to keep paying it. I don't want to lose her. If I have to kick every creepy CEO out of the building in order to keep her, then I will. And if I have to remind my partners—repeatedly—that she's a professional, then I'll do that, too."

"Okay, okay," Noah said. "We get the idea. Competent, professional, blah blah blah. Just bring her to Chicago, man. I want to meet this paragon in person. I have a feeling that if you talk about her like this, she must be something else."

I didn't answer. I let them discuss what was going to happen at the meeting next week, and as I listened, I picked up my phone and opened the text app. The call kept going as I pulled up a number and wrote a message.

Rob and Jared Egerton, I wrote. *Give me a report by Monday. The usual fee.*

I hesitated slightly before hitting Send, but only slightly. What I was about to do was ruthless, and for a second I wondered if Samantha would approve.

Then I remembered that they'd come to a business meeting and referred to her as the best pussy in New York, and I hit Send.

The reply came back in thirty seconds. *Not a problem. Done.*

Don't mess with the Man in Black, I thought, and smiled to myself as I went back to the phone call.

FIVE

Samantha

I'D NEVER BEEN a big drinker. Some of the executive assistants I knew drank a lot, and I didn't blame them—dealing with an asshole CEO all day, every day, could drive anyone to the bottom of a bottle. But I'd always kept my drinking to the occasional glass of wine, because my job was hard enough without trying to do it with a hangover.

Tonight, though, I called my sister and made her come out for drinks with me. I needed to break my rule.

I had to twist Emma's arm to meet me—not because she didn't like me, but because she was a workaholic who made a habit of staying in the office until at least nine at night. Executive assistants are driven, and they work long hours—and Emma was no exception. Twelve-hour days were the norm for me in many of the jobs I'd done, though so far Aidan had never made me work an extra-late night or a weekend.

I left the office at six thirty and took the subway uptown to our favorite wine bar on the Upper West Side. It was a tiny sliver of a place, with rich, dark wood furnishings and tasteful lighting. The wine menu was sensational, and for a few hours at least, I planned to fully enjoy it.

Emma walked in ten minutes after I did. She was wearing a jersey dress and boots, her straight, dyed-red hair pulled back into a ponytail. She put her purse on the seat next to her and didn't even bother to say hi. "Fuck," she said instead. "Fuck, fuck, fuck."

I felt myself smiling. Emma was stressed and usually wound up tight, so when she got together with me, she liked to let it all go. It would start with her sailor mouth—which she never, ever let loose on the job—and would get raunchier as the evening went on. It was like she put a lid on herself all day, and only took it off when she was with someone she trusted, like me.

"Good day?" I asked her.

"Fucking fantastic," Emma said, taking a sip of the glass of wine I'd ordered for her—the place's best pinot. "Oh, God, that's good," she said as she swallowed. "Almost as good as sex. Almost."

I sipped my own wine. "You're extra stressed, I can tell. You usually don't talk about sex until the third glass."

"What can I say? Running a successful empire isn't easy." She took another sip and sat back in her chair, looking at me. In her purse, I heard her phone buzz, and then again, as if she was getting nonstop texts. "What's up, little sis?" she asked me.

"Do you need to get that?" I asked her.

"If you want me to spend the entire evening on the phone, then sure. Remember Danielle? I've sent her on her first assignment."

I rolled my eyes. Yes, I remembered Danielle—short, pretty, the daughter of rich parents. Smart, but not very confident and incredibly needy. "You're telling me she actually made the cut?

You're getting soft, Emma. When you first started, you would have put her out on the street after the first interview."

"She impressed, me," Emma said, shrugging. "She has gumption. But she also texts me questions a thousand times a day. I'm practically holding her hand through every day at work, and if she does a shitty job, it reflects on me. It's hard to find good help these days, Sam."

My sister was the only person in the world who called me Sam. Even our parents always called me Samantha. *You just look like a Samantha,* my mother had said once. I wasn't sure if that was a compliment, but I decided to take it as one. Aidan called me Samantha, too.

And that brought my thoughts to Aidan again.

"What happened?" Emma said. "You just looked like someone killed your dog." She blinked, alarmed. "Wait. You didn't call me here to tell me you screwed up the Aidan Winters job, did you?"

"No, I didn't." Not exactly a lie.

"You're quitting?"

"No."

"You fucked him?"

"*No.*" Though I wanted to. The thought flitted through my mind, and I pushed it away again. "Jesus, Emma. I've never had sex with a client."

"Fucked," Emma corrected me. "It's after hours, so you can say the word. It's *fucked.*"

"I know the word, thanks." And I wasn't a prude. I just didn't want to say it in reference to Aidan, because he was my boss and the visuals were way, way too hot. "Still, there was a bit of a problem today, and it's bothering me. I'm not sure what the fallout will be."

Emma looked serious. In the years I'd worked for Executive Ranks, I'd never given Emma a major problem. The worst was when I'd had to leave a job because my boss wouldn't quit making sexual innuendoes at me. "Am I going to need more wine for this?" she asked.

"I wish I knew, but I don't," I said honestly.

I watched her take another sip, then square her shoulders. "Okay, go."

I'd learned something today that I never knew before: the glassed-in meeting room at the Tower VC offices had a sound problem. If you stood right in front of the meeting room door, you could hear the people talking inside. Which meant that after I'd shown the Egerton brothers into the room and closed the door behind me, I'd heard exactly what they said.

Samantha, huh? Is she single or what?

She's hot, man. Really fucking hot. I mean, that ass.

I hadn't lingered. I'd kept walking away from the door, my back straight and my ears burning. It shouldn't have bothered me —a couple of idiotic frat-boy lines, spoken by rich, spoiled men who meant nothing to me. I was a professional. It should have rolled off.

But it hadn't, because Aidan was there. They'd said those things to Aidan, as if he would get it, as if he was one of them. As if that was something he was already thinking, and they knew it.

The office door I was heading for blurred as my eyes watered, and for a second I had felt sick. We had such a careful thing, Aidan and me. It wasn't just the relationship of a boss and the underling he got to abuse. We treated each other with respect. His attitude to me was one almost of old-world courtesy, under-laid with—I had thought—genuine liking. In three months of working closely with him, I had never seen Aidan check out my tits or my ass. So I had let myself believe that he didn't think of me as a piece of office meat.

So the words, even though he hadn't spoken them, were like a slap. A reminder that I'd been an idiot. That was how men thought. *All men.* Even Aidan. Even about me.

Nine years of being the best executive assistant in New York City, possibly the country, and I was still *that ass*.

I was humiliated, and I was angry. Tears of rage blurred my eyes. If anyone had spoken to me as I did that walk of shame across the room to my office, I would have slapped them. I was used to the executive boys' club, but this one hurt. It really did.

I had reached my office when I heard the meeting room door open. I turned to see the Egerton brothers come out, their postures stiff. Jared had a smirk on his face, and Rob had his hands jammed in the pockets of his Dockers. They kept it out of their expressions, but even I could see that they were both angry, boys who were being marched out of the principal's office in front of their classmates.

Behind them was Aidan. His expression was icy and his body moved with its usual fluid grace, but he walked right behind the Egertons, as if daring them to slow down. His black suit was dark as an ink stain. He didn't look left or right, and he didn't look at me.

The Egertons were mad, but Aidan was fucking furious.

In that moment, I saw something different in Aidan. He wasn't my rich, civilized boss, the CEO of a major company. He looked sharp edged, almost rough, even though he still wore the beautiful black suit. He looked like a man who was very, very capable of kicking another man's ass.

The meeting had lasted less than five minutes. The entire office watched as the Egerton brothers walked stiffly past the reception desk and got into the elevator. When they were gone, Aidan turned and walked back to his office, still not looking at me. He was in there for only a few minutes, and then he came out again, closing the door behind him. I heard it lock with a final *click*. And then he walked to the stairwell and was gone.

The room was hushed and quiet. People were frozen in their cubicles, their jaws slightly open, their fingers hovering above their laptop keys. You could have heard a pin drop. And I still stood frozen in my office doorway, trying to understand what the hell had just happened.

Obviously the Egerton brothers had said something even worse about me, something I hadn't heard.

Aidan had kicked them out of the building.

And then Aidan had left without a word to me, or to anyone.

I took a deep breath and tried to clear my thoughts. And as I did, three things came to the surface.

First: Aidan hadn't slammed his door; he'd closed it softly, without a show of temper. Because Aidan Winters was a gentleman.

Second: I had somehow just derailed a multimillion-dollar deal by showing two men into a meeting room.

And third: I didn't know if I had a job anymore.

SIX

Samantha

I TOLD EMMA EVERYTHING. Well, everything except the part about feeling a hopeless kind of lust mixed with affection for my boss, and I left out the part about wanting to slap someone. Some things you don't need to tell the woman who gives you the assignments that pay your bills, even if she is your sister.

Emma listened intently, moving seamlessly onto her second glass of wine. "And he left for the day after that?" she asked when I finished.

I nodded.

"Have you heard from him?"

"No."

She thought it over, like a doctor arriving at a diagnosis. "Well, I didn't get a phone call, which makes sense, since you didn't do anything wrong."

"That doesn't matter, and you know it." This was why I had

wanted to talk to Emma so badly: she knew the business like I did. "What matters is that there were millions, maybe tens of millions of dollars on the table. And the deal is off because my presence disrupted it."

"The Egertons being fucking assholes disrupted it," Emma corrected me.

"They wouldn't have been fucking assholes if I had been the kind of woman they don't find attractive."

Emma swirled the wine in her glass. "It sounds like the Egertons would be assholes no matter what the circumstance."

"Emma, come on. You know your CEO clients. What's more important in their scheme of things? A single assistant or a multi-million-dollar deal? All Aidan has to do is fire me, then call you and request someone conventionally unattractive, or male, or gay. Problem solved, and he goes back to making millions. It's shallow, and it's completely unfair, but it's how the world works. Especially this world."

Emma sighed. "I've had that phone call before, I admit. The *Get me someone ugly* call. As if the men can't help themselves and they don't think they should have to. I mean, really." She rolled her eyes. "But, okay. Let's say Aidan sees your presence as the thing that derailed the deal. The fact is, he hasn't fired you."

"He also hasn't talked to me. About anything." It had been a long, long day. I'd kept my head down and kept my focus on my work, but I didn't know where Aidan had gone, or what he was doing. And, of course, it was none of my business, especially if he was upset with me.

I cared about keeping my job. I cared about my paycheck. But this job was different. I *liked* it. I could work somewhere else, but I didn't want to. I'd only been at Tower for three months, but it was already more than a paycheck. And I had a good guess as to the reason I felt that way.

What was he doing right now? Did he have plans tonight? There was nothing in his schedule. Then again, there never was.

"Okay," Emma said, her tone decisive. She pulled her phone —which had been buzzing during our conversation—from her purse and tapped quickly through something on the screen. "Here's my diagnosis. It's a tough situation, but it's made worse by the fact that you want to fuck your boss."

"What?" I gaped at her. "What does sex have to do with anything? I don't want to have sex with Aidan. I work for him. I'm a professional."

Emma kept tapping her phone, ignoring my outrage. "The word is *fuck*, Sam. You need to loosen up. You want to fuck Aidan Winters, just like every other woman in New York with a functioning vagina. It's okay to admit it, because you won't act on it. But in the meantime you'll be hung up on him and undersexed."

"I have no idea what this has to do with the fact that I almost lost my job."

"When was the last time you got laid?" Emma asked, ignoring me again.

I pressed my lips together and didn't answer.

She glanced up at me briefly, then nodded, going back to her phone. Frankly, it was a little annoying that she was only giving me half of her attention. "I thought so," she said. "Have you even dated anyone?"

"You know how dating is in this business."

She nodded again. "It's impossible. The long hours, the nonstop commitment to the job, combined with the fact that most men can't handle a woman who is successful and makes a lot of money—there's almost no time to meet anyone, and the dating pool is thin. And you can't fuck your hot boss, so you need another sexual outlet. As in, a one-night stand."

I rolled my eyes. "Emma, I haven't done that in years. Since my early twenties."

"Well, you can do it tonight."

There was a split second when my heart skipped a beat. Having sex with a stranger... Well, it had an attraction. It was dangerous, illicit, maybe hot. I wasn't about to admit this to my sister, but often when I was alone in bed with my fingers between my legs, I pictured having sex with a man I'd just met. He'd be gorgeous, and we'd barely speak, and we'd have hot, raunchy sex until I came. It was my go-to fantasy, to tell the truth.

But a fantasy was all it was. The reality was different. The reality was some guy who talked too much or told dumb jokes, or whose gaze crawled all over me, or me not knowing what to say. Then—if we even got that far—his not-so-clean bedroom in the tiny apartment he shared with roommates, who were pretending to watch TV while they listened on the other side of the wall. And if we got *that* far, the reality was awkward sex that lasted a few minutes and was completely unsatisfying. Followed by an embarrassing walk of shame past the roommates, who were still sitting on the couch. And all of that was aside from the fact that the whole thing could be dangerous if the guy was a violent creep.

The fantasy was much, much better.

I shook my head. I was twenty-nine, successful, and rational. I was going to be smart about this. "Emma, I appreciate your help. I do. And I think you're probably right that I need to meet someone. But a one-night stand is not what I need. Meaningless sex is fine, but for me it just isn't the answer."

"Mmm," Emma said, still looking at her phone. "That's too bad."

"Are you even listening to me?"

"Yeah, I am." She finally tapped her phone dark and looked

up at me. "You said that meaningless sex isn't the answer, and I said that's too bad. Which it is. Because it's too late."

"Too late? What does that mean?"

"It means I just went on Tinder and got you a date. He's going to be here in twenty minutes."

SEVEN

Aidan

AFTER THE DAY I'd had, I knew what would get me out of the funk I was in. It was the same thing that got me out of a funk every time. I really, really needed to fuck someone.

How long had it been? The last time had been a woman I'd met in a first-class airport lounge. Our flight was delayed and we spent some time talking. She told me her name was Rita, which was either a lovely name or an equally lovely lie—I hadn't cared which. When we got off the flight in Miami, she'd taken me to her hotel room near the airport. I didn't know her, and she didn't know me.

Two strangers. Completely anonymous, and only there to please each other for as long as it took to get off. That was the way I liked it.

Except I hadn't particularly liked it.

I mean, it had been fine. Me, a willing woman, both of us

naked. It had all the ingredients of a pleasant hour. There'd been physical satisfaction for both of us with minimal awkwardness. No expectations and no exchange of phone numbers. Pleasant, polite farewells when we were finished and I was dressed again.

It was my usual routine. I had never had a girlfriend, only the occasional encounter with an attractive woman. It happened a few times a year at most, when the pressure and the need became unbearable. I liked to be in complete control of my sex life; what that said about me, I had no idea.

A number of those women had made it clear they'd be open to more. *Women try to get into Aidan's pants, and Aidan says no,* Dane had said, and he wasn't entirely wrong. Most of those women would be wonderful partners—for some other man. But I was busy with my job as CEO of Tower VC, I was choosy, and I had no need to fuck all the time. It messed with my control. Besides, any woman who dated me would be in the eye of a lot of publicity, and I had no desire for wealthy divorcees, rake-thin models, or any of the other types the society pages expected to see me with.

So I kept to the routine. My sister, Ava, was the only constant woman in my life, and I only saw her when I took her for dinner a few times a year. *You're a loner, Aidan,* she'd said to me once. *Lots of guys say they're a loner, but you're the real thing.* It was how I liked it.

And yet, that last time in Miami had been... unsatisfying. Rita had enjoyed herself, but to me it had felt mechanical. Practiced. Almost tawdry. Even though I'd gotten off, I'd left as unsatisfied as I'd been when we started. Maybe even more so, and I had no idea why.

That had been months ago—nearly six months, I realized now when I did the calculation. No wonder I was so restless, unable to stay home at night, and irritable with idiots like the Egerton brothers. No wonder I was making rash decisions and fixating on Samantha's sexy goddamned shoes. No wonder I was still pissed off hours after I'd kicked out the Egertons, still so angry I couldn't talk to Samantha directly. I needed to let off some steam, and tonight I would do it the usual way.

I walked into a midtown watering hole and made my way toward the bar. I was incognito tonight: jeans, dark gray T-shirt, dark brown leather jacket, baseball cap. I often picked up women like this, so they didn't know they were sleeping with the famous Aidan Winters. Dressed like this, not a single soul would recognize me. When you were known all over town as the Man in Black, people only saw the clothes, which made it easy to wear a disguise. It was the Clark Kent effect. If I'd added glasses, I would probably have been completely unidentifiable, even to my closest friends.

But there was something else to the disguise I wore. Even though I was a success, even though I had a life that most people would envy—sometimes I chafed at being me. I wasn't born rich or powerful. I'd been a too-thin teenager from a crappy home when I'd run away at fifteen and bunked in with three of my runaway friends. We'd lived on next to nothing for years, barely staying off the streets and making ends meet. I was a different man now, but deep down I was still that teenager. I was still that kid looking for his next meal or looking for a fight. Penthouses and big offices were nice, but sometimes I needed to escape them. Sometimes I needed to be someone else for a while.

It was why I left my schedule blank most evenings and kept it to myself. The life I lived could own most of me, but it would never own all of me.

I stepped up to the bar and ordered a draft. It was mostly an after-work crowd of locals here, west of the tourist spots near Times Square and south of the upper-class bars where people would expect to see someone like me. These were New Yorkers, coming off work and letting off steam before stumbling home to do it all over again.

It was the perfect place to find a stranger to sleep with.

Because the other me, the poor me—he liked sleeping with strangers as much as the rich me did. At least, he always had.

I noticed a woman watching me from the other end of the bar. She was leaning against the bar top with one elbow, waiting for the bartender to fill her order. She had brown hair cut just above her shoulders and lightly curled. A heart-shaped face and nice eyes lined with dark makeup. A light sweater that hugged her curves. She was pretty, sexy in a rather wholesome way, and she had definitely noticed me. In other words, she was exactly what I was looking for.

It should have been perfect, but I looked away, dropping my gaze to the top of the bar. I was still thinking about the woman in Miami, about my day, about the Egertons, about Samantha. I couldn't get out of my own head.

I glanced at the woman again. She was paying for her drink, but she noticed me looking at her and met my eye. She smiled a little, in a nice way. She was probably like me: someone who didn't do this all the time, but often enough. Maybe she was getting over a bad relationship or she'd been burned repeatedly by the Manhattan dating scene. Because pretty much everyone had been burned by the Manhattan dating scene.

Did Samantha date? Or did she have a boyfriend? She'd stood in the doorway of her office, watching me as I left today. I knew I'd left her hanging, wondering what had happened with the Egerton brothers. It had happened so quickly after she showed them into the meeting room—she had to at least be curious whether it had anything to do with her. She hadn't contacted me afterward, as if she knew something was wrong. And since I hadn't contacted her, she must be wondering if she was in some kind of trouble.

Where was she right now? Pouring out her troubles on a boyfriend's shoulder? Or was she even thinking about me at all?

The thought came into my mind: *If it had been Samantha I'd met at the airport lounge that day, it would have been very, very pleasurable.*

Illogical, because I hadn't met Samantha when it happened.

If it was Samantha at the other end of the bar, we'd already be on our way out of here to fuck.

Egotistical, because it assumed she wanted to have sex with me at all. But the sex-starved mind doesn't always make sense.

The woman at the other end of the bar was looking at me again, unsure. I was still distracted by my own thoughts, and I wasn't giving her a strong enough message one way or another. She had finished paying her bill, and as I watched, the couple sitting beside her got up and left, leaving an empty seat.

An invitation if ever there was one. All I had to do was walk over and take it.

It wouldn't take much—just *hello*, some small talk, introductions. We'd tell each other things that were possibly true, possibly not. I rarely used my real name in these encounters, because I didn't want the women Googling me after we parted. If the women I met used fake names or real ones, I never knew, because I never Googled them either. It was better that way—cleaner, both of us a blank slate for a few hours, which made the sex hotter.

Except when it didn't. If I didn't like anonymous sex anymore, then what kind of sex did I like?

Samantha. In a first-class airport lounge. Suggesting I come back to her hotel with her.

In real life, she was my employee, and I wasn't even supposed to think about her like this. I tried to stop, and instead I pictured her in a blue dress—she'd look incredible in blue—and those shoes with the goddamned ankle strap. In another lifetime—one in which we hadn't met—I'd sit next to her and she'd give me a smile, her gaze going up and down me in that quick, unmistakable way women sometimes had. A once-over. And then I'd—

I blinked and realized I was standing here fantasizing about Samantha while the brunette waited, the empty seat next to her. As I hesitated, another man—brown sweater, shaggy dark-blond hair, affable smile—sat next to her and introduced himself.

She looked at me. I shook my head.

She turned to the other guy, smiled, and said hello.

Good move, Winters. What the hell was that?

I had just turned down sex. Anonymous, no-strings-attached sex—the only kind of sex I ever indulged in. I was going home alone.

All because of Samantha Riley.

I paid for my drink and left the bar. I stood on the Manhattan street, feeling the cool spring night air, scented with the unique New York fragrance of sweat, gasoline fumes, and something deep-fried. I turned in the direction of Central Park, many blocks away, and started walking.

After all, it looked like I had nothing else to do.

EIGHT

Samantha

HE SAID his name was Ethan. He was tall, with muscles he was obviously proud of because he wore a T-shirt in the cool May air. He had tattoos on his arms. He wore artfully ripped jeans and a belt with metal studs in it, and I was supposed to sleep with him.

Emma had placed herself at the bar, where she pretended not to know me. This was in case Ethan was a creep and I needed an escape. If I gave her a nod, she'd move in and extract me. If I left with Ethan, she'd leave me be.

"Hey," he said in greeting as he sat down across the table from me. I was still in my work clothes, so we looked… incompatible. Though of course that could be a turn-on sometimes. Ethan had dark blond hair in a short cut and scruff on his jaw. He was good-looking, I supposed, or at least good-looking enough to get a lot of dates on Tinder.

Damn Emma and her need to fix everything, including my

sex life. I hadn't asked her to get me a date—I'd only wanted to drink some wine and bend a sympathetic ear. But my big sister, who spent her entire career training people to make things happen, had just jumped in and taken over without asking me. Now I had a strange man sitting across from me, and I didn't know what to do.

No, that was a lie. I knew what I was supposed to do.

And if I was honest with myself, having a good-looking guy waiting for the cue to hook up with me tonight wasn't the worst problem to have. I was still young, I was healthy, and I was sitting in a nice bar, considering relieving my considerable sexual frustration.

"Hi," I said to Ethan. I smiled. He smiled back.

"Thanks for inviting me out," he said. "I know we've been messaging for a while. I'm glad you decided to meet me."

Great. That was just great. Emma had hooked me up with one of the guys from *her own* Tinder account, and he thought I was her. I darted a glance toward her at the bar, but she was innocently sipping wine and scrolling through her phone. I was going to kill her.

Still, this guy's IQ couldn't be that high, since Emma's hair was dark red and mine was dark blonde. We looked like sisters, but we weren't identical. "I'm surprised you recognized me," I said.

He shrugged. "Your photo is kind of low-res, but I can tell it's you. Though I'm not surprised you recognized me." His grin was knowing, which meant one thing: he'd been sending my sister selfies. Probably naked ones. Maybe even dick pics.

I cleared my throat. "I, um..."

"I did send a few of my face. Or weren't you looking at those?" He grinned again.

Oh, God. "I don't remember all of the pictures, I guess."

"You don't remember?" His eyebrows went up. "It was just

last night. You get that many guys sending you pictures?" He waved a hand before I could answer. "Never mind. You're hot. The hot girls on Tinder always get the most guys. I get plenty of girls, myself. It's the muscles."

Yes, he had muscles. I shouldn't have any objection to those. So why did I think that this guy—who dressed and acted tough— was actually soft compared to my boss in his sleek, expensive suit? Why did I think Aidan Winters could probably break this guy in two? I took a hefty sip of wine. "I'm glad you're successful," I managed.

"So am I." He leaned back in his chair and looked me up and down. "I can see why you didn't send me any pictures back, even when I asked for them. You're a classy girl."

"I'm not a girl, actually." The word was starting to grate on me.

"Oh, right." He rolled his eyes, and then he grinned again, as if that made it okay. "It's fine. I'll call you whatever you want. Do you want to come to my place? I'm on the Lower East Side."

Right. We were supposed to be hooking up for sex. I was supposed to be having sex with a real man instead of with my hand for once. That thought wasn't supposed to annoy me, make me think about my boss yet again. "Do you have roommates?" I asked.

"No, I have my own place, so it's private. Unless you'd rather go to your place."

His own place in Manhattan? What did this guy do for a living? It was probably in his Tinder profile, but since I'd never actually seen it, I had no idea. Besides, what did it matter what his job was? This was supposed to be anonymous sex. The hot kind. The less I knew about Ethan, the better.

"So, Emma," he said, grinning at me. "What do you say?"

There was something about that—him calling me by my sister's name—that did me in. I could have sex with a stranger. I could even do it if he didn't know my real name. But I honestly couldn't fuck a man who thought I was my sister. It was just too weird.

This wasn't going to work.

"I have to confess something," I said to Ethan.

His eyebrows went up. "Confess what? You're into kink? I'm open to anything."

"I'm not actually Emma," I said. "I'm her sister, Samantha. Emma is over there." I pointed at the bar, where Emma was sitting. Ethan looked, too. Emma's lips parted and she stared back at us, busted.

Ethan still didn't get it. "You want me to fuck both of you?"

Jesus. "No," I said. "My sister was trying to set me up, but I don't think it's going to work." I pointed. "She's the one who has seen your pictures, not me. I think she's the one you should work on."

He could have been mad. I wouldn't have blamed him; he'd been brought here on false pretenses. Instead he stared at Emma without glancing at me again. Emma stared back.

"Okay then," Ethan said.

I sighed. I was going home alone.

As Ethan stood and walked over to the bar, I put money on the table and gathered my purse. It was a little humiliating, even though the entire situation was absurd. I'd just been dumped for my sister, even though she should have been out with the guy in the first place.

I took one last glance at the bar. Ethan was leaning against it, talking. Emma was her usual cool self, but she was smiling.

Everything was so easy for her. Have a problem? Fix it. Want to start an uber-successful company? Do it. Need to get laid? Message a guy whose dick you've already approved and get on with it.

I wouldn't even be able to hold a grudge against her for

tonight, which she knew perfectly well. Despite this annoying stunt, my sister was the one person I counted on in this big, heartless city. Truly, she was my only friend.

As I walked out the door onto the cool, dark street, now lit with lights from signs and traffic, I thought about Aidan Winters. He was my friend too, perhaps. Someone I counted on. He'd probably find that absurd, which it was—he was my boss, and I was self-reliant anyway. I could see him now, giving me one of his wry looks and saying *I think I'm flattered, Samantha, but I'm not sure.*

I still didn't know if I was fired for derailing the Egerton deal.

I didn't know if Aidan was my friend or not.

I didn't know where he was right now. With a woman, maybe. Talking, laughing. Fucking her. Maybe a woman he saw regularly, maybe one he'd just met. I didn't know what was in the blank parts of his schedule. It was none of my business.

I turned and walked up the street toward the subway, wondering if he was ever as lonely as I was.

NINE

Aidan

THE NEXT FEW days kept me busy, and I was rarely in the office. It sounds like a ruse, but it wasn't; my specialty at Tower VC was real estate deals. Real estate deals require looking at lots and lots of real estate. That's the job.

In fact, I'd spent more time behind my desk over the past three months than I had in a year. I'd put off plenty of showings and appointments all over town, just so that I could spend more time at the office. The reason was Samantha Riley. She didn't know that, and it was best if it stayed that way. In the meantime, I had a business to run.

We were in touch constantly, even when I was traveling from appointment to appointment, all over New York. She kept my schedule, sorted my email, filed my paperwork, drafted letters, dealt with HR and the legal team. We texted frequently and talked on the phone several times a day. She was as competent and intelligent as ever, figuring things out before I had to take the time to tell her, anticipating problems and killing them before they could arise. I turned down three deals in three days, but I also closed one. A deal that would make a lot of money. My professional life was made easier, and more profitable, because of my paragon of an executive assistant.

It was hell.

I didn't see her first thing every morning. I didn't hear her voice or see her smile. I didn't get to catalog what she was wearing every day—the dark gray pencil skirt? Or had she moved to lighter spring colors? Was her hair worn up or down? She usually wore it up, but she varied the style. She'd worn it down only a few times since I'd met her, so it wasn't her usual style. I wondered why that was.

Aside from my selfish desire to look at her, I sensed something else was wrong. Samantha was more reserved than before—she was always professional, but this was different. She was almost stiff, and sometimes when we talked on the phone I felt like she was trying to get rid of me. As if she didn't want to talk to me at all.

It festered. It had something to do with the meeting with the Egerton brothers, I was almost sure of it. I had walked out without a word to her that day, but I'd never done anything to give her the impression that the problem was with her. I'd simply been too furious to say anything at all. It was my old, teenaged temper rearing up; usually I conquered it, but not that day. I'd been too angry. But I was calm now, and I'd figured that if the topic was never mentioned, Samantha would get the idea that nothing was wrong.

It had backfired somehow. She stopped joking and making small talk. She was all business.

On Friday afternoon, I figured out why.

I was in the office to meet with two of the lawyers from our legal team to go over contracts. Since they were Tower employees, I didn't need Samantha to greet them at reception or show them in. Since it was almost the end of the day, I didn't need her to furnish coffee or food. I let Samantha work in her office, and I met the lawyers in the meeting room myself.

I had forgotten a few papers on my desk, so I left the meeting room to go get them. As the door closed behind me, I heard one of the lawyers say, "That guy scares the shit out of me."

It was as clear as if he'd said it in my ear. Something about the acoustics sent the sound straight to where I stood instead of muffling it, even though the door was closed.

I blinked in surprise for a second, and then I remembered the Egerton brothers, saying their frat-boy bullshit as Samantha walked away. I hadn't looked closely enough, watched her body language as she walked. If I had, I probably would have seen her stiffen—because she'd heard.

I walked away from the meeting room and headed straight for her office. I didn't think twice about what I'd heard—*that guy scares the shit out of me.* Scaring people wasn't something I set out to do, but if I had that effect, fine. It could even be useful.

Besides, I didn't care what the lawyers thought. I cared what Samantha thought.

Her office door was open and she was sitting behind her desk, typing at her laptop. She sensed me coming and looked up as I approached, her eyes wide.

"In my office," I said. And then, because that sounded harsh, I added, "Please."

Samantha nodded and stood. I heard her follow me the short distance to my door. The lawyers could see us through the glass of the meeting room. They might be wondering what was happening, but I'd forgotten about them.

When we were both inside my office, I didn't round the desk and sit down. Instead I closed the door and caged her against it with one arm, letting the other drop. She backed up against the door, bumping into it in her surprise. Her lips parted.

"You heard," I said.

"What?" she asked.

"When the Egertons were here. You heard what they said."

She blinked, and the surprise left her eyes. I was so close I could watch her quickly calculate, the thoughts moving swiftly. "I heard some of it, yes," she said, her voice cool.

"That's why you're pissed at me."

"I'm not pissed at you."

I searched for different words. I was so close to her, I could smell her delicate scent. Words weren't coming easily with that scent in my nose. I'd shrugged off my jacket in the meeting room and loosened my tie, and being in my shirtsleeves in that moment felt almost naked. "You're not talking to me," I tried again.

"We're talking right now."

Her chin was up, her eyes sparked with quiet defiance. Still, even though I had one of my arms at my side, she didn't make a move to get away. "It isn't the same, and you know it," I said. "Something's been wrong for days."

"Why would you think that? You've barely been here."

Were we fighting? I couldn't tell. "I had things to do."

"I know. I keep your schedule. Which was suddenly very full."

"Do you have something to say about my schedule, Samantha?"

"Only that everything became quite urgent as soon as I was worried I was about to get fired. You'd rather avoid me than talk to me about it."

I looked into her eyes. They were blue, but not a searing blue —more of an understated shade. Her makeup was understated, too, mascara and liner and a light, flattering shadow. My sister was a fashion stylist, and I knew plenty about how women made themselves up. Samantha did it expertly, just as she did every-thing expertly. I'd never been close enough to see her precise magic before.

"You thought you were going to get fired," I said. It wasn't a question. Her words had hit me like a punch in the gut.

She blinked once, looking at me with a trace of scorn. "Of course I thought it. You were set to make a multimillion-dollar deal. Then one of the Egertons made a remark about my ass, and the whole thing was off."

"That's what you heard? The ass remark?"

Again, her expression was subtle, but it was there. A wince I was close enough to see. This got to her somehow. Got right under her perfect skin. "Yes," she said.

So she'd walked away before she heard anything else. "Let's get the truth out, then," I said. "He also called you the best pussy in New York. And he said he'd do you."

She winced again, harder this time. The words hurt her. Oh yes, the Egerton brothers were going to pay. She didn't speak.

"Does that bother you?" I asked her, not letting up.

"I'm used to it," she said. "It means nothing."

"It means nothing, yet it's bothered you for days."

"The words don't bother me," she gritted out. "It's the fact that..."

"That what?"

"That he said them to you."

It was like a slap to the face. I had a sudden understanding of what was wrong with us, and I wanted to rip my own guts out to undo it. "You thought I'd welcome them talking about you like that," I said. "You thought it would be fine with me."

"For a second, yes."

"And it hurt your feelings?"

"Yes, and it made me angry." She paused, thinking about it. "Furious, actually, because it hurt."

I felt my hand twitch at my side, but I made myself stay calm. "And then?"

"And then you kicked them out, and I wondered if I'd get fired."

"Fired for doing nothing but your job?"

That trace of scorn again. "Life isn't fair, Aidan. If you'd done the deal, Tower would have made a lot of money. So in a way, I cost you millions."

Money. She thought I gave a fuck about money. Well, maybe she could be excused for thinking that. I certainly made a lot of it. "Okay, you want to talk, I'll talk," I said. "No one, and I mean no one, talks about you like that to me. I don't care who it is. If Steve Jobs comes back from the dead and calls you a piece of ass, I'll kick him out of this fucking building. Is that clear?"

I heard her slight intake of breath, and she nodded.

I gestured briefly to the door behind her. "If anyone out there gives you any shit, they're finished. If anyone makes comments about your weight or the way you dress. If any guy asks you out when you don't want him to. My tolerance is absolute fucking zero. You say you're used to it, but you aren't used to it if you work for me." I made myself say it. "That includes from me. I don't look at you or talk to you that way, and neither does anyone else."

She paused for a moment, and then she nodded. She had so much composure, this woman. "Thank you," she said, her voice calm.

"You're welcome," I said. "You can go home for the weekend whenever you want. I'll see you at the airport on Monday, when we go to Chicago."

TEN

Samantha

BY MONDAY, I was a wreck. I tried not to show it; I tried to be calm, professional Samantha Riley. This trip to Chicago should have been routine. After all, I had been on plenty of business trips in my career, sometimes alone, sometimes with my bosses.

None of those men were Aidan Winters.

In the months I'd worked for him we'd only ever been together in the office during business hours, with dozens of people around. We'd never been alone; we'd never even done lunch. Aidan had never suggested it. After the conversation—or was it an argument?—we'd had on Friday, I wondered if that was because he didn't care to have lunch with me, or because he didn't want me to feel uncomfortable.

My tolerance is absolute fucking zero. That includes from me.

I'd thought a lot about those words as I went about my weekend. They resonated in my brain as I shopped, cooked, did laundry, went to yoga class. I held Warrior One in the tiny, trendy studio I went to at 40th and Tenth, listening to the instructor talk about oils and heart chakras, and I heard Aidan's voice in my head, saying those words. I thought about how those words made me feel.

They gave me the shivers. I'd never had a boss who took how I was treated so seriously; the usual attitude was *It's a tough business, so get tough or get out. I don't have time to listen to your complaining.* And I was tough—I could fend for myself at work, and I had no problem speaking up. I didn't need Aidan to defend me. Still, the fact that he was willing to—that he actually had— made me weak in the knees.

But it was the second emotion I felt at those words that threw me for a loop. Because I was disappointed.

I was all the way to Savasana, staring at the ceiling, when I realized why. It was because he'd said *I don't look at you or talk to you that way.*

And deep down, I wanted him to.

Even though Aidan was my boss, even though I worked for him in a job for which I was eminently qualified, part of me wanted him to want me. Sitting in the quiet of the yoga studio, I could admit it, at least silently to myself.

This was very, very bad. I hated that Emma was right. I hated that I finally had a boss who treated me with actual respect, and *I didn't want him to.* I hated that I was so hypocritical that I expected Aidan not to stare at my ass, yet I had the urge to stare at his. I hated that I spent my yoga class thinking about his hands and his sexy jawline and the ruthless look in his eyes that turned me on. I hated that the idea of traveling alone with him, staying in hotels with him, made my heart skip a beat. I hated that the one man who made me hot was the one man who had set down an inalterable, unbreakable rule that he would never touch me.

I walked home from yoga class in a terrible mood. In my

apartment, I tossed down my rolled-up mat, stripped, and had a shower. Then I got into bed naked, slipped my hand between my legs, and pictured Aidan Winters until I came so hard I saw stars.

Afterward I stared at the ceiling, just as frustrated as I was before. Then I got up and made dinner.

*

ELEVEN

Samantha

I WAS at the airport early, but Aidan was earlier. I walked to our gate at La Guardia to see Aidan already there, sitting in one of the hard chairs, his laptop open on his lap. He was somewhat casual, but he was still the Man in Black: he wore black jeans and a black sweater, expensive and molded perfectly to his body. He was clean-shaven, his gaze fixed on the screen in front of him as one hand absently rubbed his chin. He didn't notice me until I stood in front of him.

He looked up at me and blinked. He'd been so engrossed he was surprised to see me. His dark eyes quickly took in what I was wearing, then looked back to my face again. Right. Because he wasn't supposed to be looking at me.

I was wearing loose linen-blend pants and a dark gray tank top. I had ballet flats on my feet and a slouchy cardigan wrapped around me like a shawl, my hair tied up in a ponytail. It was an outfit meant to be comfortable on a cramped airplane, with the extra layer for the plane's cold air. As an added bonus, it was an outfit that covered all body parts without being fussy or easily wrinkled. It was rather different than what I usually wore to the office, and for a second I wondered if he liked it or not.

Then I remembered I didn't care.

"Samantha," Aidan said. "Hello. Did you have a nice weekend?"

I remembered my Sunday afternoon orgasm indulgence, thinking of him, and fought the urge to blush. "It was fine, thank you. And you?"

His schedule for the weekend had been blank, as it usually was. Aidan's off hours were still a mystery. "It was very restful," he said vaguely, then gestured to the seat next to him. "Make yourself comfortable. We board in forty minutes."

"What's so fascinating?" I asked, taking the seat next to him and putting down my bags. "You barely noticed my existence just now."

"I always notice your existence," he said, though his tone wasn't flirtatious. He paged through the document on his laptop. "This is a report I asked for."

"From who?" It wasn't a nosy question. I knew every report due to Aidan, and when it was due. It was my job to make sure every one of them was submitted on time. I'd seen nothing come into his email inbox, so this must have come to his personal account.

"No one you know," Aidan said, frowning a little. "More of an external thing."

"Oh." I crossed my legs and pulled my purse onto my lap. This was fine; we were fine. Everything was fine. Just a girl and her boss in the airport on a business trip. Friday—whatever that had been—was in the past. My strange thoughts of yesterday were in the past. This was business.

I was digging in my purse for my phone when Aidan held up a hand. His watch was silver and black and gorgeous, and it glinted against the soft wool of his sweater. "Okay, okay," he said with aggrieved humor. "I'll tell you if you'll just top badgering me. I can't take it anymore."

I smiled. "I knew I could make you give in."

"You can." He frowned again. "Truth be told, it's a report about the Egerton brothers."

I put my purse down and looked at him. "The Egerton brothers?"

"Yes. Specifically, their history." He clicked through a few more pages. "This was originally a revenge thing for me, but now I'm finding interesting information."

I stared at him. My hands had gone cold.

He looked away from the document and at me. "I suppose you should know this about me, Samantha," he said. "I am not a very nice person, especially in business. You're going to learn that, since you're going to be meeting my partners."

I blinked, my eyes dry. Revenge. He was talking about revenge for someone making a comment about my pussy and my ass. "You mean because your partners know you so well," I said.

Aidan nodded. "We've known each other since we were fifteen. I suppose you've heard the story of how Tower VC was started?"

"Dane Scotland invented a database software, and you sold it for millions of dollars."

"Forty-six million, to be exact. We were twenty-one. I don't know much about software, but what Dane created had something to do with making databases easier to crawl and access, even across multiple platforms. Very big databases. So a company like Apple, for example, could look at what was selling in every store across the country—updated by the minute."

"Impressive," I said.

Aidan smiled. "Dane's mind is impressive. The rest of him is a little rough around the edges."

I nodded. I'd never seen a photo of Dane Scotland. He was based in Chicago, and he wasn't a gossip media darling like Aidan was. "What about the others?" I asked.

Aidan scratched his chin. "I'll give you the honest answer, I suppose. Noah is our partner in L.A., which works for him because he is deeply devoted to sleeping with models and movie stars. Alex is our Dallas partner. He's the only one of us with a criminal record."

My lips parted in surprise, but I tried to keep my composure. "Oh?"

"He was eighteen," Aidan said. "He was in a fight that went wrong and got too violent. Unfortunately, that fight was with his own brother."

"I see."

Aidan smiled again at my politeness. "We all grew up in Chicago. Our home lives were difficult in different ways, for different reasons. When we left home, we moved in together in a run-down old apartment that cost us four hundred dollars a month. We lived there while we finished school, and we all worked menial jobs while Dane built the software. When we sold it, we used the money to start Tower VC. The rest is history."

I thought about that, four teenaged boys living in an old apartment that was better than home, trying to make a better life. "It's a good story," I said.

Aidan shrugged. "My point is that even though I have money now, it doesn't change my roots. I've fought for everything I have, and I'll keep fighting if I have to. I may wear nice clothes, but I basically come from nothing."

"I know that feeling," I said. "I come from nothing, too. Though I also come from something."

He raised his eyebrows at me. "Please explain."

I bit my lip, hesitating. It wasn't a story I told many people. But I had the urge to tell it now. "You know my sister, Emma? I think you met her when you hired Executive Ranks."

Aidan nodded.

"Well, Emma and I are adopted. We were found abandoned outside the doors of a hospital. I was a baby, and Emma was one."

"Jesus," he said softly.

I nodded. "From the way the story was told to me, we weren't hurt. It didn't look like we were starved or abused. We were just... left." I let out a breath. "Anyway, we were adopted together by our parents—our adoptive parents—and they took good care of us. Emma and I grew up in a safe, loving home with parents who wanted us. So that's what I mean when I say I came from nothing, and also from something."

He was watching me, his dark eyes unflinching. "I'm glad it turned out so well for you. But it must be a strange piece of your life, not knowing who your parents are."

He'd gotten right to the heart of it, as usual. "I love my parents. And they handled it the right way, telling me about the adoption when I was ready. But it makes me think differently about myself, I think. I've had to make my own identity, create who I am, in a way that others don't. I've spent a lot of time wondering what parts of me are me, and what parts of me are my biological parents. If any parts are me at all."

I'd never spoken like this to anyone, but Aidan didn't flinch. "I know that feeling," he said.

I wanted to hear what he meant by that, but they called us to board the flight. We took our seats in business class, and Aidan went back to his laptop, the conversation apparently over.

I thought about working, too—I *should* work. I had lots to do.

But somehow, unburdening myself had made me both light-headed and exhausted. Just a few words, a few sentences, bottled up for so long and finally spoken aloud. It made me feel like I'd climbed uphill at a run.

I laid my head back against the seat, and I was asleep by the time takeoff was finished.

TWELVE

Aidan

CHICAGO WAS COLDER than New York. It was a little bit uglier, a little harder, and these days it was more dangerous and less touristy. It still felt like home.

Samantha was quiet on the drive to the hotel. She'd slept soundly through the entire flight—maybe unburdening herself to me had tired her out. I hadn't minded, because she looked good even when she slept in an airplane seat. Besides, I hadn't wanted to talk about my own history. I also hadn't wanted to talk about what was in my report about the Egerton brothers.

I'd read the report twice over during the flight, and it was very juicy, but I was distracted. I kept thinking about what Samantha had told me, picturing her and her sister abandoned on a hospital's steps. Anything could have happened to two tiny, defenseless girls. The world was shit. I owed their adoptive parents a thank you.

Not that I'd ever get the chance to give them one, since Samantha's personal life was none of my business.

My phone rang as we pulled up to the Four Seasons. It was Noah. "I just landed," he said when I answered. "Are we drinking or what?"

I glanced at Samantha, who I knew could totally hear what Noah was saying in the quiet of the car. "It's one o'clock in the afternoon. On Monday."

"So that's a yes, then."

"We can meet," I allowed.

"You are so fucking uptight," Noah said. "You always have been. Do I have to convince you to come drink?"

"It isn't me you need to convince," I said, wincing to myself because Samantha had doubtlessly heard the *uptight* comment. "It's Dane. He's the recluse. He's been working on something big and he doesn't want to leave it. He won't want to go."

"Dane will fucking go," Noah said. "I'm calling him next." He hung up.

I put my phone down and looked at Samantha. The car had pulled up to the hotel, and the driver was getting out to open her door. She smiled at me, amusement in her blue eyes.

"You don't have any brothers, do you?" I asked her.

"No."

"Well, you're about to see what it's like. My partners aren't my blood brothers, but they may as well be. Would you like to come for a drink?"

WE CHECKED IN, and as I was cleaning up in my room, my phone rang. It was my sister, Ava.

"You went to Chicago without me?" she said. I'd texted her this morning, telling her I was going and that I'd say hi to our mother for her. With anyone else, that would be a simple message. With Ava and me, it was a sarcastic joke.

"Be honest," I said to her. "Would you have come?"

She huffed a breath. Ava lived in Brooklyn and was a fashion blogger and stylist. She may have been born in Chicago, but New York was in her blood and she had no desire to go back. "I would have thought about it."

I sat on the edge of the bed. "It's for work, anyway. It isn't a social trip."

"Are you really going to see Mom?"

"I'm sort of obligated, aren't I? I should at least check on how she's doing."

Ava was quiet for a minute. She was four years younger than me, and the scars from our childhood ran deep. Making a better life for Ava was part of the reason I'd run away from home; when my partners and I had our apartment, she had always been welcome to stay, and she'd bunked with us often instead of going home. "I tried calling her a few weeks ago," she said. "She told the nurse she didn't want to talk to me because she doesn't have a daughter anymore."

I shook my head, even though Ava couldn't see me. "She doesn't mean it. You know that."

"I know it's the illness. And yet, deep down, she kind of does mean it. Because the illness makes her more honest than she used to be."

"That's how she is. It's how she's always going to be."

"I know. I'm in therapy because of her. I've come to terms with the fact that my mother may be mentally ill, but she's also a bitch."

"Is that the word your therapist tells you to use?"

"No, I think the term is *emotionally unavailable*."

"That sounds accurate."

"It also means *bitch*."

I laughed. It was a very, very dark joke, the kind that only Ava and I would get. The kind of joke you would only understand if you'd been raised—and I used that word loosely—by Laura Winters.

Ava was one of the few people on the planet who could make me laugh. She was blonde, at least for now, and she was outgoing —the complete opposite of me. Underneath the frothy exterior she was a focused career woman who had made a fashion blog and a flair for style into a very profitable business, but she didn't like to admit that part. She liked to tease me that my all-consuming love of money was beneath her artistic sensibilities. "Well, I'll drop in and make sure our mother is still alive, at least," I said. "I'll be sure to report back."

"Better you than me," Ava said. "What's the business in Chicago, anyway? Did Dane's coding finger break?"

Ava knew my friends from those years when she'd stayed at our apartment. Hanging out with four smelly, uncouth teenage boys, with their mountains of mess, was better for Ava than being with our mother. It was fine with us. Ava was never one of the boys—she wasn't a tomboy, and she'd been a fashionista even then —but she was fun, hard to offend, and tough enough to take our jokes. We were all protective of her, and she put up with us most of the time.

It was Dane, though, that she liked to tease. Dane was our computer brain, our coder, and as a teenager he'd looked...well, like a nerd. Glasses and ill-fitting clothes made up his whole look. He was also surly and had limited social skills. He was Ava's favorite butt of jokes, even now.

"Dane is fine," I said.

"Maybe he left his computer and saw sunlight for once. I could see how that could be traumatic." She was on a roll now. "Or a real live girl talked to him? God, he might have passed out."

I rolled my eyes. "You haven't seen Dane in a long time, you know."

"I know. It's been years, and his picture isn't plastered all over the New York gossip sites, unlike my brother. Are you saying that Dane actually bought a new shirt sometime over the last few years? One that doesn't smell? I'll believe it when I see it."

"You can make all the jokes you want, but he can't actually hear you. You know that, right?"

"True, but it's fun making them anyway. Are all of the boys there?"

"We are. We're about to meet for drinks."

"Oh, that actually sounds fun. Though the testosterone might be too much for me."

"You're not used to it anymore. It won't be all testosterone. My executive assistant is coming, too."

"Which one is this? The new one? Samantha, right?" I didn't talk to many people, but it was impossible to keep anything from Ava. "I hope she's ready."

"She'll be fine." But as I said my goodbyes to Ava, I thought it over. The Tower VC boys were a lot to handle sometimes. Well, I'd told them to behave. I'd just have to hope they listened to me.

THIRTEEN

Samantha

WE MET at a bar called Caponi's, a few blocks from the hotel. The Chicago spring air was brisk, and it was windy—appropriate, I supposed, in the Windy City, though no native Chicagoans ever called it that. It wasn't exactly warm yet, but people were out in their spring outfits, happy that the long, icy winter was over. There was nothing as optimistic as Chicagoans in early spring.

I wore a navy blue sweater dress and knee-high boots, my hair in a ponytail. Aidan met me in the lobby—he had changed out of the sweater and replaced it with a black button-down shirt, open at the throat, and a casual black jacket. My sister Emma was right —my boss was an absolute snack. Damn it. And this felt disturbingly casual, so as soon as we started walking I talked business.

"There are plenty of emails piling up," I said. "If you want me to deal with them back in my room while you meet your partners, I'd understand."

"Are you chickening out?" Aidan asked, sounding amused.

"Not at all. I'm just trying to figure out the situation. You hired me to work for you, but apparently we're going drinking in the middle of a Monday afternoon."

"You don't have to drink if you don't want to."

"I know." I hadn't decided about that yet. I was nervous enough to crave a glass of wine, and at the same time alcohol seemed like a bad idea. These were very important men, and I needed to make a good impression. "I'll work later tonight to catch up."

"You don't have to do that, either." Aidan paused, and something seemed to occur to him. "Do you actually think I'd invite you out during a weekday, then blame you for not being up-to-date on your workload?"

I laughed. "I can tell you've never worked for any other CEOs."

"That's an asshole move."

"And your point is?"

"Jesus." He was thoughtful for half a block. I noticed a couple of women staring at him, but he seemed oblivious. "Can I ask you something?" he said as we approached the door to the bar.

"Sure," I said, though I wasn't.

"Do you like working for me?"

It was such an unexpected question that I couldn't think of an answer for a second. "Yes," I said, though I didn't say the rest of it—that this was the best assignment I'd ever had, that I wanted to please him, that I wanted to make this work. "Yes, I do."

He stopped outside the door and turned to look at me. "So you'd like to continue working for me," he said. "Long term."

I nodded. "Yes, I would."

"Then this—" he gestured to the door of the bar, where his

partners were inside "—is important. My partners need to know you, and they need to trust you as much as I do. They need to know that any aspect of the business can be turned over to you without question. And the first part of that is for them to meet you, preferably casually, so they can see who you really are. So if it helps your psyche, then look at what we're about to do as work."

He was right. We might be having a drink, but these men would have the power to promote me—or fire me. I might be Aidan's assistant, but my job meant that the other partners had to trust me, too. A question occurred to me. "Why don't the others have assistants? Why only you?"

"Because Dane is too grumpy, Alex is too secretive, and Noah thinks he already has everything figured out."

I really needed to meet these guys. I crossed my arms and looked at Aidan. "Okay, boss, you've convinced me. I'll have a drink."

He smiled. My knees went wobbly, but I didn't think he noticed, because I covered it up pretty well. "Thank you, Samantha," he said. "Let's go."

THE FIRST PERSON TO approach Aidan when we walked in was a tall, broad-shouldered, gorgeous man with short, dark blond hair. He was wearing jeans, a white button-down shirt and a dark brown leather jacket, and he flung one arm over Aidan's shoulders as if they'd already been drinking for hours. "The Man in Black has arrived," he said. "Now we can *really* have fun."

I'd never seen anyone touch Aidan, let alone grab him like that, but Aidan didn't seem to mind. "Samantha," he said to me, "this is Noah Pearson."

"I know Samantha," Noah said before I could answer. He

dropped his arm from Aidan and held out his hand for me to shake. "She's the only one who answers my emails."

I felt myself smiling. I could see this man, as Aidan described, dating gorgeous actresses nonstop. Obviously he was making the most of his life in L.A. But he was charming, and he certainly was handsome. His handshake was warm and firm, too. "It's nice to meet you in person," I said.

"Come in and have a drink," Noah said. "The others are here."

He led us back to a table. The bar was narrow but deep, reasonably busy even for a Monday afternoon, and it smelled of crisp beer and something salty. I suddenly wondered if they had good food. I'd had nothing but airplane snacks all day.

At a table at the back were two more men. One was big and rough-looking, bearded, corded with muscle, his brown hair tied messily at the back of his head in a man-bun. The other was leaner but deadlier-looking, with dark hair and a black T-shirt from which tattoos snaked out of the sleeves and down his arms. Neither of them looked like they belonged on the board of a venture capital firm. One of them must be Dane Scotland, the genius computer programmer who had built the original software that launched Tower VC. Neither of these men looked like a computer geek either. Then again, Aidan had described Dane as "rough around the edges."

"Gentlemen," Aidan said as the two men looked at us. "This is Samantha Riley, my executive assistant. Samantha, this is Alex Blake." He gestured to the dark, tattooed man. Then he gestured to the big guy with the man bun. "And this is Dane Scotland programming wiz."

"It's nice to meet you," Alex said as I pulled out a chair and sat. He had a shadow of dark beard on his jaw. With his tattoos, black tee, and dark hair, he looked a little dangerous, but his eyes were kind. The hand that shook mine was adorned with silver rings. "Dane," Alex said. "Say something nice to the lady."

"I can be nice," Dane said to Alex. He looked at me. "Hi."

"Hi," I said.

"Dane's manners need work, but don't worry," Alex said. "That means he likes you."

"My manners are fine," Dane said. He looked at Aidan. "Where's Ava?"

Aidan had pulled out the chair next to me and sat in it. I felt the heat of him, his vitality, his familiarity. "Ava is my sister," he said to me. "She lives in Brooklyn." He turned back to Dane. "She didn't come. This is a business trip. Or at least that's what Noah said."

"It's absolutely a business trip," Noah agreed from his place at the end of the table. "I have an investment you'll all be interested in. But we'll talk about that tomorrow. Tonight, we catch up."

"I haven't met your sister," I said to Aidan.

His features went a little soft at the mention of her, which told me she was a favorite person of his. It made me curious about her immediately. "You might meet her," he said. "She comes into the city often enough, but she hates coming to the office. Be warned, though, that if she meets you, she'll dress you. It's nothing personal, or a commentary on how you dress. She's a fashion blogger and stylist. It's just what she does."

"Does she dress you?" I asked.

That made Aidan smile. "I've learned plenty of tricks from her, but I dress myself."

"Can't you tell?" Alex said, grinning at me.

"The Man in Black," Noah said. "Haven't you ever wondered why black is all he wears?"

I looked around the table, then back at Aidan. He shrugged good-naturedly. "Yes, I wonder," I said. "Everyone wonders."

"It's so that he always knows what color to buy," Alex said. "That way, he doesn't have to coordinate."

I turned to Aidan, shocked. "Is that true? That's the reason?"

Aidan scratched his chin. "I hate clothes shopping," he admitted. "If everything I buy is black, it's just easier."

All of the gossip and the speculation. Aidan's reputation as a remote, slightly sinister legend. The nickname of the Man in Black. Not because Aidan was a villain, but because he was too lazy to coordinate his wardrobe. "I'm seeing you in a whole new light," I said.

He narrowed his eyes at me. "I do own other clothes. You've just never seen me wear them. Now, how about a round of drinks for the table?"

FOURTEEN

Aidan

"I KNEW you'd pull that shit," I said to Noah later as we stood at the bar, getting drinks. Back at the table, Samantha was eating nachos and listening to Alex tell a story while Dane silently sipped his beer. She seemed to be relaxed and having fun.

"Pull what?" Noah said innocently.

"Telling her my secrets."

"Well, I happen to know you're shit at color coordination. It won't do to have her thinking you're perfect. Which she probably does."

"No," I said, thinking of the shitshow last week. "She doesn't think I'm perfect."

He picked up his beer. "She's very pretty, by the way. Beautiful, actually."

"I'm sorry?" I cupped a hand to my ear. "Can you repeat

that? You said you'd like me to rip your balls off and play hockey with them?"

"Relax. I'm not going to make a move on her. She's not my type."

"Too classy?"

"Too smart. Too serious." He shook his head. "The kind of woman who actually wants you to stick around. No, thanks."

I could criticize Noah's sex life, but then again, at least he knew the real names of the women he slept with. At least he was having sex at all, unlike me, who had suddenly lost the ability—or the desire—to pick up an available and willing woman in a bar.

I glanced at Samantha. Was that the kind of woman she was? The kind who wanted a man to stick around? She was so polished, so careful, that it was hard to tell, but I had the feeling there was something else beneath the surface. Something a little rough and very, very sexy. If only I could figure out exactly what it was.

No. I wasn't going to do that. Right. Out of the question.

"She's a very valuable employee of mine," I told Noah sanctimoniously. "I'd rather not talk about her sexual proclivities, thanks."

He swigged his beer. "God, you're as uptight as ever. I've seen you so drunk you puked, you know."

"I was seventeen."

"What does it get you, though? Living like there's a stick up your ass?"

Noah knew nothing about the women I picked up, the things we did together. The less he knew, the better. "I don't have a stick up my ass. As for my reputation, you should take a look at the Tower balance sheets sometime. My reputation as the ice-cold Man in Black scares everyone and gives me the advantage in business deals. It makes us a lot of money."

Noah shook his head. "Maybe, but I couldn't do it. Be someone else all the time. Play a role."

No, that wasn't Noah's style. He was who he was, flaws and all. "Then it's good you're manning the west coast office and not New York," I said. "Leave New York to me."

"Gladly," Noah said. He picked up his beer. "I'm going back to rescue Samantha from the awkwardness of sitting alone with Dane."

I glanced at the table. I couldn't see Alex, and Samantha and Dane were sitting together. Dane scratched his head, then said something brief. Samantha smiled and said something polite back.

Jesus, Dane really needed to figure out how to be in a social situation. He didn't look like a geek anymore—laser eye surgery, a gym regimen, and lack of a haircut had done that job—but deep down he still was the computer nerd who coded for fun. No wonder he never got laid.

Noah headed back to the table and a hand clapped me on the shoulder. It was Alex, coming to the bar to get his own drink.

"I like her," he said to me without preamble. "She's cool."

"Good, because she's going to know everything you know about Tower VC. Probably more."

"Fine with me." Alex shrugged and pushed his empty glass toward the bartender, motioning for a refill. "You know I'm not the paperwork guy. I can already tell she has me beat on smarts. It doesn't take much, to be honest."

That was a lie. Not the paperwork part—Alex was allergic to paperwork. But he had a brain. He just didn't use it, preferring to hide behind the prison record and the tattoos. You'd think Alex would be out of place in Dallas, but he wasn't. He would have been out of place in New York or L.A. Strangely enough, the cowboys and ranchers liked Alex quite a bit. Alex was tough, and Texans appreciated tough people.

Most people only saw the ex-con, dark and possibly danger-ous, but I'd known Alex a long time. I knew the damage that drove him, the scars he had that wouldn't heal.

"Do you ever hear from Kat?" I asked him.

Alex pulled his fresh drink across the bar toward him. It was a whiskey, neat. He'd definitely spent too much time in Texas. "No," he said, his tattoos flexing as he raised the drink and sipped it. "We're divorced, remember?"

Kat had been Alex's high school sweetheart. Back in those days, he was a rough teenager with a shitty home life, and Kat was the best thing in his life. They adored each other. She'd even stuck by him through his eighteen months in prison, waiting for him when he got out. They got married at twenty-one.

Then it all went to shit. None of us knew exactly what happened—Alex wasn't talking. But Kat moved out and Alex got hard. Really hard. He got in more trouble. He lived alone in a big house in Texas, and he did oil and ranching deals with very hard men for Tower VC. He didn't wear suits, he didn't take orders from anyone, he didn't date. And he didn't talk about Kat. Ever.

Alex took another sip of his whiskey and looked at me. "So what do you think Noah dragged us all across the country for? This deal he has in the works?"

"I have no idea," I said. I watched Noah sit down next to Samantha, say something to make her laugh. Had I ever made her laugh?

If he kept doing that, I was going to kick his ass all the way back to L.A.

Alex watched where my gaze was fixed. "He's such an asshole," he said.

I didn't have to ask who he was talking about.

Alex finished his whiskey. "He's an asshole, yet I wish I was more like him. Don't you?"

FIFTEEN

Samantha

WHEN I ROLLED over in bed the next morning, the first thing I felt was pain. I put a hand on my forehead. It wasn't a hangover—I'd had exactly one glass of wine at the bar yesterday afternoon while talking to the Tower VC partners. Then I'd come back to my room and ordered room service—no alcohol—while I caught up on work before going to bed.

Yet as I pushed myself up from the pillows, a second bolt of pain throbbed through my head, pulsing behind my eyeball. I groaned. I sometimes got migraines, but it had been months since my last one. I didn't need to get one now.

I rifled through my suitcase and took some ibuprofen. I shuffled to the bathroom and washed my face, hoping this wasn't actually happening. In the mirror, my eyes looked exhausted and bloodshot, and my skin looked gray. I groaned out loud, miserable in my beautiful luxury hotel room.

I checked the time. It was 8:30. I was due at the Tower VC Chicago office at nine, and I wasn't even showered or dressed. How had I slept so late? I had a vague memory of waking up earlier, then falling asleep again. Or had I imagined it? The pain descending on my skull was so intense I had a hard time thinking.

I walked back to the bedroom, looking through my suitcase for a full minute before I remembered I had hung my work clothes up in the closet. I was standing in front of the closet, thinking in panic about a shower, when there was a knock at my hotel room door.

"Samantha? It's me."

Aidan. Coming to pick me up and take me to the Tower VC office for the meeting—the *very important* meeting—with all the partners. The meeting I was supposed to be at so I could impress all of them with my capable professionalism, and I was standing in my sleep shirt, bewildered and in pain. A moan of excruciating panic left my throat.

"Samantha?" He sounded alarmed now. He must have heard me. Was my moan that loud?

"I'm coming," I managed. The words were weak in my throat, but I got them out. I walked unsteadily to the door and opened it.

Aidan stood there, beautiful in his usual black suit and tie. His eyes went wide as he took me in.

That was when I realized two things: I was in a pair of panties and a tee and nothing else, and I was about to throw up.

"Um," I said.

He stepped into the room and closed the door behind him. "You're sick," he said, putting a hand on my elbow to steady me. He put his other hand on my forehead, testing for fever. "Is it the flu?"

"Um," I said again. Nine years as New York's best executive assistant, and I couldn't even talk. The pain was lancing down the back of my skull to the back of my neck, and forward where it throbbed behind my eyes. I closed my eyes, feeling his competent hand on me, keeping my balance. "Migraine," I managed.

"Jesus," he said softly. His arm came around my waist and he gently held me up as he led me to the bedroom. "It looks fucking awful."

"I'm okay," I said, which was a pathetic joke. I was not okay. I was a mess, and it was happening in front of my favorite boss, the one I wanted to impress, the one I was attracted to. It was so humiliating. "I don't want to throw up," I said, the words unbearably loud inside my skull.

"Lie down," Aidan said, his voice low. I crawled gratefully between the cool sheets and he pulled the covers over me. He went into the bathroom, where I heard the water run. Then he came back and put a cool towel on my forehead. It was only a few degrees of relief, but I sighed.

He moved around again, this time adjusting the dark curtains and the lights. The world stopped spinning so hard. I pulled the cool towel over my eyes, partly for relief and partly so I wouldn't have to look at him. "The meeting," I said.

"You're not going to the meeting." His voice was deliberately soft. He came back to the bed and put his hand on the side of my neck. "How often do you get these?"

"A few times a year." I nearly whispered it. His hand felt so good. He smelled so good. I wanted him to crawl in bed with me, suit and tie and all, and lie here with me. I would feel better if he did that. I always dealt with my migraines alone. "I don't know what brought it on."

"Could have been anything." His hand—so warm and strong —moved to the back of my neck and his fingers pressed gently there, moving at the base of my skull. "Does this help?"

For a moment the pain pulled back a little, like a wave at the beach, and I moaned.

His fingers paused. "Samantha, I don't know if that's a good moan or a bad moan."

Even through the pain, I felt a pulse of heat between my legs when he said that. "It's a good moan," I managed weakly. Oh, God, we were talking about me moaning. He had most likely seen my panties and my nipples through my shirt when I opened the door. I'd never wanted him to see me weak like this. "I'm so embarrassed," I whispered.

"Don't be." His fingers moved again. It wasn't complete relief, but made the pain recede just a little. "How long will it last?"

"An hour our two." I hoped.

"Is there anything I can do?"

"I need quiet. The maids…"

"They won't come. I'll make sure of it. Are there any drugs you can take?"

I'd been through this with my doctor. Nothing worked. "No. I just have to wait."

He kept the massage up, bless him. It was faint relief, but it was relief. "I don't know what to say," he said after a moment. "Think of something pleasant, maybe. Something that makes you happy."

My answer was immediate, even through the pain. "Paris."

"Paris is your happy place?"

"Yes. I've wanted to go there for as long as I can remember. I feel like if I was there, I'd be…different." I sighed. The pain was making me stumble to find the right words. "I feel like I could be someone better there. Someone who could live a great life. Which is crazy for a place I've never been to. It's hard to explain."

"No, I get it," Aidan said, his fingers still blessedly moving. "Sometimes you glimpse what life could be like. It isn't that the life you have is bad. It's just that certain places are like looking through a window into what could be."

That was exactly it. Exactly. I felt like crying for a moment—

the pain was making my emotions go crazy. "Yes," I managed. "That's it."

"If you feel that strongly about Paris, then you're probably right about it." He didn't seem to notice I was near tears.

"Maybe." I sighed. "What's your happy place?"

Aidan laughed softly. "Probably the Met. Not quite as exotic as Paris, I know. But I live near it, and I go as often as I can."

"You do?" I'd kept Aidan's schedule for months, and there had never been mention of the big museum on the edge of Central Park. I'd only been there a few times myself.

"Do you want to know a secret?" Aidan said. "Everyone wants to know what I do in my spare time. They think I should be snorting drugs or flying jet planes or fucking models. But usually, in my off hours, I'm looking at art. I don't know why. I'm not artistic in the least. I have no talent myself. But looking at art makes me happy. Art, for me, is that thing that shows me what life could be."

I let his words wash over me as his fingers rubbed my neck. How was he so stupidly perfect? "That's lovely," I managed. Then the pain seized the top of my skull like a pincer, and I winced, my hands gripping the coverlet.

Aidan's voice was laced with concern. "Do you want me to stay?"

"No." I said it forcefully, because I did want him. I really, really did. But the CEO of Tower VC couldn't miss a meeting with his partners because he was busy rubbing his assistant's neck. The idea was ridiculous. "Go to the meeting, Aidan. I'll be fine."

He sat for a moment, still rubbing my neck, thinking it over. Was he actually considering skipping his meeting? Eventually he said, "All right. But I'll get a copy of your key from the front desk and take it with me. I'll check on you in a few hours, and I don't want to knock. If you want me to bring anything, text me."

On impulse I raised my hand and grasped his wrist, my grip weak. "Thank you," I said.

The massage stopped. For a second we sat there, Aidan sitting on the edge of my bed, his hand cupped behind my neck, my hand on his wrist. I still had the cloth over my eyes—there were circles of exploding pain in the darkness—but I could hear him breathe. I could feel his pulse under my fingertips.

Then he gently pulled away and stood. I heard him walk to the door and leave without a word.

I lay there in the dark, thinking about Aidan asking the front desk for my key. They'd give it to him. He was Aidan Winters.

His scent was still in my nose, crisp and masculine. I didn't need the cloth off of my eyes to know it. I'd know it anywhere. I wondered if his skin smelled like that.

Except to shake my hand the day he met me, he'd never touched me until today.

I lay there, thinking about Aidan, smelling Aidan, as I waited for the pain to subside.

SIXTEEN

Aidan

"YOU'RE LATE," Alex said.

The four of us were standing on Michigan Avenue. All around us, the warming sun of spring glinted off the skyscrapers. It was a quarter past nine, and the heading-to-work crowds were moving fast, a little panicked. Behind us was the building that housed the Chicago office of Tower VC—we rented a few offices on the sixteenth floor, where our staff worked and where Dane worked when he could be persuaded to come to the office.

"Samantha is ill," I said.

Alex's eyebrows went up. "Was it something we said?"

I shook my head. "Migraine. She says she'll be fine in a few hours."

"Migraines are bastards," Alex said. He was wearing a suit today—dark blue, with a white shirt and a light blue tie. Next to him, Dane sipped a coffee, wearing jeans and a black hoodie, his hair in its customary man bun. On the other side of Dane, Noah —impeccably dressed in a gray suit he'd likely imported from Italy—checked his watch, then looked at the street.

"Here he comes," he said.

We were waiting for the car and driver Noah had hired. Instead of meeting in the office, I'd had a text telling me to meet the others outside on Michigan Avenue, and we'd be taken to this amazing, once-in-a-lifetime investment opportunity of Noah's.

I hadn't had time to think very much about what Noah wanted us here for. Noah did his part in L.A., but he rarely came up with new ideas for Tower VC. He knew how to navigate his own waters, but he was the least ambitious of us. And he almost never got excited about business projects—Noah worked to live, instead of living to work. I looked at him as the car pulled up and wondered what had him so excited now.

Normally I would have extracted every detail from him by now, because I hated surprises. But I'd been too distracted by Samantha to pay attention. And this morning—Jesus. Distracted was an understatement. It was fairer to say I was thrown completely off my game.

The Samantha I knew was competent, unshakeable, put together in every detail. The woman who opened her door this morning was a raw, exposed nerve, exhausted and—yes, I could fucking say it—helpless. She'd hated that helplessness, but there was nothing she could do about it. When I'd put my arm around her waist, she'd sunk into me, soft and pliant, leaning on me.

I didn't have a thing for helpless women. Some men have a white knight fantasy, but that wasn't me. The women who attracted me were confident and pretty clear on what they wanted from me. No, helpless women didn't turn me on. Except for this particular helpless woman.

It was only a few days ago when we'd agreed there would be no crossing of professional lines. Yet this morning I'd put her into bed, watching every perfect curve slide under the sheets, carefully not staring at those high, soft breasts under her T-shirt. I'd wanted to take her pain away any way I could, even if it meant blowing off this meeting and getting into bed with her, holding her until she felt better again.

Except I knew that if I did that, as soon as the headache was gone I'd pull down her scrap of panties, go down on her, and pleasure her until she came. And *then* I'd sink into her, feeling her every quiver and breath, and I'd fuck her deep and slow until the pain was forgotten and she came again, squeezing me.

And that would ruin everything.

I still wanted to fucking do it.

Way to be an asshole, Winters, I thought as we filed into Noah's hired car. *She's your assistant. You're about to gleefully destroy the Egerton brothers for talking about her ass.*

I ran a hand through my hair. *Because it's mine,* I thought, *or it should be. It should be fucking mine.*

"All right," Dane said, breaking into my fog of thought. "Where the hell are we going, Noah?"

Noah looked him up and down as the car pulled into Michigan Avenue traffic. "I told you to dress for an important meeting."

Dane shrugged. "This is how I dress for important meetings."

Noah rolled his eyes. "Should I be glad you at least aren't wearing the Duran Duran T-shirt you wore the entire year you were sixteen?"

"It was vintage," Dane said. "Besides, it doesn't fit me anymore."

It wouldn't. Dane hadn't gained weight, but he'd bulked up since he was a teenager, and a lot in the past few years. He said that working out relieved his boredom, but I had the feeling Dane finally got tired of being the scrawny, nerdy programmer. The current version of him could get women by the dozens if he tried, but with his fuck-off personality he *still* never got laid.

"Okay, fine," Noah said. "You can dress like a slob, but keep your mouth shut and let me do the talking."

"Done and done," Dane said, looking almost pleased.

"Hey," Alex said, looking out the window. "This is the old neighborhood."

I looked. He was right. We were in the South Side, and we'd come to the neighborhood we'd lived in years ago. All four of us had been born within a mile of here; the house I grew up in was only six blocks away, though there was nothing there for me anymore. No memories, no family, nothing.

Then it hit me. "We're going to the old building," I said. "Our place."

There was silence in the car. Noah didn't deny it.

I looked at him. His handsome, open face was quiet now, almost solemn.

At fifteen, all four of us had left home. We all had different reasons. My mother was a single mother working two jobs, who wanted me out of the house. Alex's father was hitting him. Dane's parents had pretty much forgotten about him. And Noah had rich parents who hated him.

Noah had talked the school janitor into telling the landlord that he was Noah's father, that the rest of us were cousins, and that it was all on the up-and-up. He'd signed the papers, and Alex had promptly learned how to forge the janitor's signature anywhere else we needed it.

We lived in that apartment for seven years. It was in a shit neighborhood and it was nothing to write home about, but we loved it. And sure, we were four teenage guys who didn't have much money and weren't particularly clean. The place was still home until Dane's software made us rich, we started Tower VC, and we moved out to spread across the country.

"What are we doing, Noah?" I asked as all the familiar buildings slid by outside the window, all the familiar streets. "Why are we going back to the old place now?"

Noah scratched his chin, but finally he answered. "Because the entire building is for sale," he said. "And we're going to buy it."

THREE HOURS LATER, I let myself into Samantha's hotel room. I was tired and drained in a way that had nothing to do with sleep. The trip down Memory Lane had been good, bad, and everything in between.

Noah was right: our old place was for sale. Not just the apartment we'd rented, but the whole building. It was in even worse shape than it had been in when we left; it needed updates, upgrades, and renovations. Probably several million dollars' worth. The real estate itself was going for next to nothing, but that didn't mean the place was cheap.

The cost didn't matter. If the building wasn't bought, it was going to be condemned. Noah wanted us to buy it, renovate it, put the Tower VC Chicago offices on the top floor, and rent the rest out.

It was a nice idea. It was also an idea that would lose money—lots of money. Which was the opposite of what a venture capital firm is supposed to do.

We'd debated it for over an hour, sitting in a diner long after the real estate agent had left. Noah said the money didn't matter. That was typical Noah, who liked to roll the dice and hope for the best. The problem was that the rest of us liked money—a lot. We'd worked fucking hard to earn what we had, and Tower VC was built on Dane's genius, Alex's muscle, and my sales and finance acumen. It was easy for Noah to dismiss money when it was the rest of us who had made him rich without his parents.

And at the same time, he was right. Tower had a healthy bank account and access to almost unlimited loans. This one project, as expensive as it was, wouldn't sink us. And if we didn't buy the building, it would be gone. A piece of our past, reduced to rubble.

"We can't let that happen," Noah said. "Fuck the money. Let's save it."

Alex had crossed his arms. "I didn't get into business to lose money on a bunch of sentimental shit. You want a keepsake, go buy an old record or something. I'm out."

Dane voted for the project. He was a Chicago boy to the bone, and he didn't want to see a piece of Chicago condemned.

I voted against it.

We were at an impasse.

Samantha's room was dim and quiet. Nothing had been moved or rearranged, so she hadn't been out of bed. There were no room service dishes, so she hadn't eaten, either.

I walked softly to the bedroom. My assistant was still in bed, sound asleep, but she'd been tossing and turning. The covers were pulled out and twisted, and one long leg lay across the top of the coverlet, sleek and almost unbearably sexy. Her shirt was twisted up, exposing her smooth hip beneath the cotton of her panties. Her hair was tangled in the pillows, her face slack. The migraine had obviously receded, and now she was sleeping it off.

I wanted to touch her. I wanted to slide my hand up her bare leg, over the perfect curve of her ass. I wanted to wake her up with my cock pressed against her, my mouth on her nipples. I wanted to do every fucking dirty thing to her, and then do it all again. And again.

Samantha was my assistant. My employee. My just being here was completely wrong, crossed every line. For God's sake, I was in her bedroom, watching her sleep. Fantasizing about fucking her. On a business trip.

Somehow we'd gone from professional colleagues to something very, very dangerous. Something neither of us should want any part of.

And still I wanted to get into that bed with her. I ached to do it.

I took a step back. I was bigger than this, smarter than this. I was a man who managed his sex life with ruthless precision, who had his desires under cold control. I could stay out of my assistant's bed and treat her with respect instead of fucking her senseless. Everything about this was wrong.

That was the reason I liked it. But what I wanted didn't matter. *Get a grip, Winters.*

I left the bedroom and put her key card on the table next to the door. I slipped out of her room, closing the door silently behind me, and walked down the hall to my own room.

I walked to the minibar, poured myself a slug of Scotch, and downed it. In my pocket, my phone vibrated silently—a message. I had my ringer off. It was my private number, the one that very few people were in possession of. I pulled out my phone and checked who had called.

It was the hospital where my mother was currently a patient. Because after years of not caring for Ava and me, my mother was losing her mind, irrevocably, piece by piece. And putting her in the hospital was the only thing I could do.

She'd been a single mother to me and Ava when we were growing up. Our father had hit her—Ava and I were too young to remember—so she'd left him. She'd worked long hours at a factory and left us alone much of the time. Not her fault, but even when she was home, we were treated like an annoyance. *Be quiet. Go to your room. Go play. Go to bed. I don't have time.* When I was ten, I'd heard her tell the woman next door that she wished she'd never had kids. *Some women just aren't made to be mothers,* she'd said. *That's me.*

At fifteen, I'd packed a bag and moved in with my friends. My mother had never told me to come home.

It wasn't exactly a loving upbringing, but I'd survived. It was harder for Ava. Ava was the one who needed affection, who craved it. Who just wanted someone to love her. That person wasn't going to be our mother. We could wish things were different, but it was never going to happen. As adults, there wasn't much my sister and I could do about it except get therapy—in her case—and soldier on.

And then, a few years ago, our mother had been fired from her job for absent-mindedness. She got pulled over and her driver's license had lapsed because she'd forgotten to renew it. When the traffic cop asked her questions, she looked at him in confusion because she thought he was her cousin Garrett.

She was young, the doctors said, for that kind of deterioration. But it wasn't unheard-of, and there was no treatment. Maybe someday there would be, but not now.

So now, at thirty-four, I paid for the care of the woman who had barely acknowledged me for twenty years. I visited her when I could. Sometimes she remembered she had a son, and sometimes she didn't. Sometimes I thought she only pretended not to remember.

I'd called the hospital earlier to arrange a visit before I left Chicago. Now I checked the message they'd left. *Mr. Winters, we're very sorry, but today is not a good day to visit your mother. She has said that she doesn't want to see you.*

"Fuck you," I said to no one in particular. Not my mother, who couldn't help who she was and the sickness that was taking her. Not my partners. Not Samantha. Maybe I was saying it to God. Or to myself.

I hung up the phone. I could drink; I could spend the evening jerking myself raw, thinking of Samantha in the room a few doors down. I could get pissed and feel sorry for myself. But I had a better idea.

I pulled out my suitcase and started to pack. It was time to go back to New York.

SEVENTEEN

Samantha

AS THE PLANE APPROACHED LAGUARDIA, I closed my laptop and put it away. I ignored the empty seat beside me, where my boss was supposed to be sitting.

It was Thursday. Aidan had left Chicago sometime while I slept on Tuesday, leaving me a simple text: *Gone back to New York. Hope you feel better. I'll be in touch. Enjoy your day off. A.*

Of course, the first thing I wondered was whether his change of plans had something to do with me. Was he upset that I got sick on the day of the partners' meeting? Then I realized that was egotistical and ridiculous. Aidan was a powerful man who could, and did, do anything he wanted. None of his decisions revolved around me.

We had corresponded since by text and email, and everything seemed fine. I had taken his advice and enjoyed my day off yesterday, spending the day with my parents in their small suburban bungalow, watching golf and talking gardening with my dad, going shopping with my mom. They had cooked me a big dinner—Dad fired up the barbecue—and fed me to bursting. All in all, it had been a great day.

Aidan had said he would take the day off, too, to visit family. But he'd gone back to New York instead. I wondered why—but that was none of my business.

As the plane taxied toward the terminal, I pulled my wrap around me and tried to push down the flutter of unease in my stomach. My migraine was long gone now, but there was no doubt it had been a weird moment between Aidan and me. I remembered the way it had felt when he put his arms around me —the texture of his fine wool suit against my thin T-shirt, the warmth of his body underneath. I remembered how he had smelled, the line of his clean-shaven jaw. I'd never been that close to him before. In the moment, I'd been afraid of throwing up, but thinking back on it, I could remember the details now that I wasn't under a fog of pain and humiliation.

He'd put me in bed. He'd rubbed my neck. I'd put my hand on his wrist.

And he'd come back to my room sometime when I was sleeping and left his copy of my key on the table.

All of it made things awkward now, to say the least. How were we supposed to work face-to-face?

Maybe we would just move on, ignore what had happened. That was probably best. We were boss and employee. The neck massage while I was wearing nothing but panties and a T-shirt could fade into the past where it would hopefully be forgotten.

I winced to myself, standing up to grab my bag from the over-head. There was no way I was forgetting that, even if Aidan did. I'd remember the feel of his fingers massaging my neck forever. Talk about embarrassing.

You're a professional, Samantha. Act like one.

I could. I would.

And if I wanted my boss's hands all over me, rubbing more than just my neck, then I'd just have to suffer.

AS IT TURNED OUT, I didn't have to worry about how Aidan and I would work together. Because he was avoiding me.

He had back-to-back meetings out of the office the first day I was back. Then he flew to Atlanta for a meeting. Everything was done by email and text, the messages concise and impersonal. Polite. He flew to Denver for another meeting. A week in, I got the idea. We were going to pretend that Chicago never happened, and we were going to do it by never being in the same room again.

It was exactly like the time after the meeting with the Egerton brothers. Obviously the Man in Black had some hang-ups when it came to talking to his assistant directly. Okay, last time I'd avoided him a little bit, too. And maybe I had been letting it slide for a week because it was easier. But it still made me angry. I hadn't done anything wrong in Chicago, and neither had he. We hadn't done anything together. Nothing at all.

Absolutely nothing, when I wanted to do so much.

Another week passed, and I didn't see my boss. He took meetings in New Jersey and Washington, and when he was in Manhattan he came in to the office at some ungodly hour and left before I got in. Then—I realized when I saw the timestamps on his emails—he'd come in again after I left for the day, and he worked into the evening. All so that he wouldn't have to be in the same room with me.

It was ridiculous. It didn't matter that the work of Tower VC got done just as efficiently as it ever had; it was still stupid. It had to stop.

So one Friday night, I left work at six. I pretended I was going home, but instead I went down the street to the bookstore and browsed for an hour, picking out a novel to read and buying it. Then I walked back to the Tower VC offices and let myself in.

The office was dark and empty except for a beam of light coming from Aidan's office. His door was ajar and his desk lamp was on. I crossed the open office space and stood in his doorway.

Aidan was sitting at his desk, his laptop open in front of him. He was wearing his customary black, though his jacket was flung over a chair, his tie was loosened, and the top two buttons of his shirt were undone. He heard me coming, and his dark gaze fixed on me.

There was a second of vertigo as I looked at him. He looked good, but he wasn't as put together as usual. His hair was mussed slightly, and there was a shadow of beard on his jaw, as if he hadn't shaved in a few days. The cuffs of his sleeves were roughly rolled up. The effect was so hot it made my knees weak. I did my best not to let on.

"Good evening," I said to him.

What was Aidan's expression as he looked at me? Anger? Annoyance? Something else? He wasn't happy to see me, and he didn't pretend otherwise. "Samantha, what are you doing here?" he asked bluntly. "It's seven o'clock on Friday night."

I crossed my arms. I was still wearing my trench coat, my purse and the bookstore bag slung over my shoulder. "It seems this is the only time I can get a meeting with my boss."

He scowled. "If you needed a meeting with me, you should have scheduled one."

"Would you have come?"

"What kind of question is that?"

"Come on, Aidan. Ever since Chicago, we've been acting like two divorced parents who have to trade off the kids every weekend."

A muscle in his jaw ticked. "Nothing happened in Chicago."

There was a second of silence, heavy and thick. I pictured his hand on the back of my neck, his fingers moving over my skin. I knew he was picturing the same thing.

"I agree," I said. "Nothing happened in Chicago."

His voice was harsh. "Then why are you angry with me?"

"Because I haven't seen you in two weeks."

"We're not married, the last I checked."

God, he was being an ass. I rolled my eyes. "I'm aware of that, and I thank God for it, believe me."

Aidan pushed his chair back, laced his hands together over his stomach. Those hands. His strong wrists. My gaze dropped to them, and I pulled it away by force, made myself look at his face again. That was no better, because now I was looking at his cheekbones, the line of his mouth. The stubble on his jaw. Wondering what it would feel like on my skin.

"I don't see a problem," Aidan said. His voice was icy cold. I'd heard him use that voice in meetings when he was particularly annoyed. Most of his employees shook with fear when he used that voice.

"Then you're blind," I said. Never, in my entire career as an executive assistant, had I ever spoken to a CEO like this. It had never even crossed my mind. Yet with Aidan, the words came out. "If you don't want me to work for you anymore, just say so. It can be a mutual agreement."

"Why the fuck wouldn't I want you to work for me?" Now he sounded angry. "When the fuck have I ever said anything of the kind?"

"Does this kind of thing work on your other employees?" I asked him. "Acting one way, then pretending the other person is crazy? Well, you can play your game if you like, but you'll be playing it alone. If you can't acknowledge a problem, then I'll do it myself. And I quit."

I turned away from the door, lightheaded. I hadn't intended to quit. It wasn't my plan. But there was no way I could work for a man who couldn't be in the same room with me. I couldn't even blame him entirely—it was hard for me to be in the same room with him, too. I wanted him so badly, and I couldn't have him.

I started across the dark open office space, trying not to wobble as I walked. Behind me, I heard Aidan's chair move, his laptop snap shut. The lamp went off and his door closed. His legs were longer than mine, his stride faster, and in seconds he had caught up with me. "Samantha. What the fuck?"

Normally, Aidan didn't swear when he spoke to me. Now he couldn't seem to stop. "I was clear, I think," I said. I kept walking.

His hand touched my elbow. It wasn't rough—it wasn't even a grab—but my body stopped as surely as if he'd spun me around. That was how much control he had over me without trying. When I looked up at him, his dark eyes were blazing.

"You are not fucking quitting," he said.

"You have no say in it," I told him.

"Yes, I do."

"No, you don't." I turned again, moving harshly, even though he wasn't holding me. Because it felt like he was.

As I moved, my bookstore bag fell to the floor, the book I'd bought spilling out. Before I could stop him, Aidan had stooped and picked it up. He looked at the title, at the back, and I felt my cheeks get hot. I'd bought an erotic romance, this one particularly dark. The title was *One Night with the Devil*, and the cover featured a photograph of a woman's elegant hands, bound at the wrists with a thick red silk ribbon.

Aidan turned the book over, looking at the back. I knew he was seeing the words *taken* and *possessed* and *unimaginable pleasure*. I knew he was seeing the words in bold: *I barely knew him, yet I couldn't resist his command.* The author's name was Melina Cherry.

I stood there with my hands clenched, refusing to feel ashamed. I was a grown woman, and I could read whatever I wanted. "Give that back," I said.

He handed it to me. He didn't scoff or laugh; he didn't even have a derisive look in his eye. Instead, he looked at me with the same intensity he had before. "Is that how you get off?" he asked. "With books?"

That was tonight's plan. I was pent up and wanted an orgasm, but that was none of his business. "Would you rather I do it with strange men?" I snapped, shoving the book back in the bag. "Would that be more acceptable to you?"

He looked furious, and for a second my breath stopped. "It isn't acceptable to me at all."

I made my voice work. "Well, that's too bad. Once again, you don't get a say."

"I know I don't." Aidan stepped forward, closer to me. I didn't step back. I could smell him, that deep, masculine scent, and this close I could see the stubble on his jaw. I clenched my hands again so I wouldn't touch it. "Do you know why I've been avoiding you?" he asked me, his voice low with anger.

"In fact, I don't. Why don't you enlighten me?"

His jaw flexed. "I've been avoiding you because in Chicago, I wanted to fuck you raw. That's why I left. That's why I've stayed away from you."

The words hung there, stark and dirty. I couldn't breathe.

"You wanted it, too," Aidan said. "You can say you didn't, but you would be lying. Now who's pretending that problems don't exist?"

My lips parted. I wanted to deny it, but I couldn't think of a single thing to say, because I couldn't lie. Not now. Not to Aidan.

I put the book away and rubbed my hand over my face. "Aidan, we have a problem."

"It's only a problem if you quit."

"We can't work like this."

"We can, because you're not going anywhere."

I dropped my hand and shook my head. "I don't see how it can work. We can barely be in the same room. How are we supposed to work together? It's better if I leave."

His voice was a growl. "You are not leaving."

"It isn't because I want to," I admitted. "I don't. I like the job. I like the company. I even like you, when you're not being an ass."

"I'm rarely an ass." He sounded so fucking sure.

I looked up at him, at his gorgeous face in the shadows of the darkened office. I'd missed his face. I could admit it. Seeing Aidan was one of the things I looked forward to every day. The first thing I looked forward to every day, to be honest. Not setting eyes on him for too long had made me unsettled and cranky.

And now, if I left, I wasn't going to see him anymore. Not ever again, unless I looked him up in the tabloids.

"Samantha," he said gently, as if he was reading my mind.

"Do you know what I think?" I said, the honesty coming out of me again. What did I have to lose? "I think that if you and I were different people, in another place, in another lifetime, this story would have had a different ending."

Aidan blinked, something flitting behind his dark eyes. "Different people," he said.

"Yes." I looked away, thinking of the book in my bag, of the characters. I felt my cheeks go hot again. "If we were just... someone else. Both of us. But we're not."

He was quiet for so long that I looked at him again. To my surprise, he didn't look angry anymore. Instead, there was a spark of something devilish in his eyes.

"What?" I said.

"We can be," he replied. "Different people, I mean."

I thought of the book again. Then I remembered my real life, the one I lived every day. It was a nice dream to be someone else, but it wasn't possible. "We can't be different people," I said. "Not forever."

Aidan's voice was almost harsh. "Who said anything about forever? We'll do what the book suggests. You and me. But not you and me at all."

It hit me, what he was saying. What he was suggesting. *One Night With the Devil.* The idea started deep in my belly, like fire, and then my whole body felt warm.

Being someone else—someone entirely different—for a little while. One night. With Aidan. Was that the game?

One Night with the Devil.

We were silent for a long moment, looking at each other. I knew he could see my flushed skin, my dilated pupils. I knew he could hear my hurried breath. I'd had so many fantasies about sex with a stranger. If we did this, it would be like living out the fantasy. Except the stranger would be Aidan.

I could think of a million reasons it was a bad idea. But I still couldn't think of a way to resist.

"It would have to be... for a little while," I said at last. "And then it would end, and we'd be ourselves again."

"Agreed." Aidan's voice was low and quiet now. He said one more word. "Tomorrow."

Saturday. I had no plans, except to sit home with my dirty book and fantasize. Why do that when I could do the real thing? "Yes," I said.

Aidan nodded. He lifted a hand and touched his finger to my jaw—just the lightest brush, as if he couldn't help himself. It lit my skin like fire.

"Wait for my instructions," he said, and then he was gone.

EIGHTEEN

Aidan

I WAS STRANGELY CALM, all things considered. I went home to my penthouse and changed into my workout clothes. I went to the gym in my building and did my usual routine of running and weights, pushing myself until I felt my muscles rip. Then I went back to my place, drank a protein shake, and showered.

I hadn't planned the idea I'd sprung on Samantha, but as soon as it surfaced in my brain I knew it was right. Don't get me wrong—the idea of the two of us shedding our identities in order to fuck was screwed up, and many people would likely disapprove. But it was the right idea for Samantha and me. I'd seen the certainty of that reflected in her eyes.

I liked to be with strangers. It seemed she liked the same thing.

Except this plan had a built-in failsafe. We already knew

each other and—I hoped, at least—somewhat liked each other. We'd had three months of familiarity and a buildup of trust. For me, I wasn't risking a night that I likely wouldn't truly enjoy, with a woman who might demand more than I was willing to offer. And Samantha? She had more to risk than I did. A night with the wrong stranger could be embarrassing or humiliating at best, dangerous at worst. Women walked a tightrope that men never had to think about. With the plan I'd laid down, Samantha would get to play, yet know she was safe at the same time.

And she'd obviously liked the idea.

I wasn't too worried she would get cold feet and change her mind. Samantha was nothing if not smart, confident, and brave. She wasn't a pleaser and I'd never seen her waffle over a decision. She had a cool determination that most women would give a limb to have, which was one of the many reasons she was at the top of her profession. And in a work setting, I very much admired her calm.

Saturday night, though, I planned to break it.

I had come out of the shower and was drying myself off when my phone rang. It was the private detective I'd hired to look into the Egerton brothers.

"I got the payment," he said when I answered. "Thanks for being so prompt. It's what makes you one of my best customers."

"You're welcome," I said, scrubbing the towel over my hair and dropping it on the bed.

"You sure you don't need anything else? There were definitely a few unexpected pieces in the info I found. I can keep digging if you want."

"No," I told him. "I'm done. I'm going to drop it."

"Really? That isn't like you. I got the idea this was some kind of revenge thing."

"It was, but I've thought better of it now. I'm going to let the matter rest."

He sounded disappointed. Some of the tidbits he'd found really were juicy. "If you say so, Aidan. What are you now, forty? I think you're getting soft in your old age."

"I'm thirty-four, and fuck off."

He laughed. "Have a nice weekend."

"I plan to." I hung up and looked at the phone.

I had lied when I said I was going to drop it. I had no intention of doing any such thing, but I didn't want his services anymore. It doesn't pay to have any one person know too much about you, especially if you're hiring them. People you're paying can always be bought by a higher bidder. It isn't a fault of theirs, it's just the way people are. You can't buy loyalty, which plenty of ancient kings and current Mafia dons could probably tell you.

However, you don't need paid loyalty when you have friends like mine. I thumbed through my numbers and dialed Alex.

"Howdy," he said in a fake Texas accent when he answered, because he knew it sounded absurd and that it drove me crazy. I pictured him back in Dallas, sitting in his top-floor apartment, alone like I was.

"Are you bored?" I asked him.

"Always," he replied. "Tell me you're going to amuse me."

"I have a side project if you're willing to take it."

Alex knew me well, so it took him only a beat to catch on. "Does this have something to do with the Egerton brothers?"

"Bingo."

"You gave a good impression in Chicago of having moved past being angry about that."

"I'm an excellent actor when I need to be."

"Damn, you are cold." He sounded pleased. I heard him take a sip of something. "Go ahead."

Here's the thing: Alex was the only one of us with a prison record. He wasn't a career criminal, but he did have a certain willingness to cross lines that the rest of us couldn't or wouldn't cross. He knew people the rest of us didn't know. Even as a teenager, Alex knew things like how to hotwire a car or how to spot an undercover cop patrolling our shitty neighborhood. He knew which guys on which corners sold what, even though none of us ever bought anything. When we first rented our apartment together all of us were underage, which meant none of us wanted to get caught up in the system. Knowledge was power, and Alex had a natural talent for the right kind of knowledge.

"I'm going to forward you the report I got," I told him. "There are a lot of details, but the basics are that the Egerton brothers possibly stole the original code for their stupid, multimillion-dollar app from a rival six years ago."

"Why doesn't that surprise me?" Alex asked.

"Probably because you have an IQ to speak of."

"That's information that could make their investor value tank right before their IPO."

"Certain people would see it that way, yes."

"And where is the former rival now?"

"That's the funny thing. At first he tried to sue. It got pretty far, but then the case was dropped. No settlement or legal agreement. It was just dropped and the man moved to Florida."

"Maybe he likes beaches and malls. I hear it's beautiful there."

"Maybe a thirty-year-old programmer is a little out of place amongst the retirees."

"Sounds like an interesting theory. Why don't you pay your investigator to dig him up?"

"Because I don't completely trust him," I replied. "Because this has to be done right, which means no leaks. Because I want this guy dug up, and I don't really care what means are used."

Alex took another sip of whatever alcohol he was drinking. "Let me get this straight, Aidan. You're asking me to leave my very important position brokering deals for Tower VC and go to

Florida, so you can take completely insane revenge on two guys who made comments about your assistant's ass."

"And her pussy," I said, because I was still pissed about it. "Otherwise yes, you're correct. Come on, Alex. Doing oil and ranching deals has you bored out of your mind. You want a challenge."

He was quiet for a second, and then he said, "What I want, apparently, is some alligator repellant and a mosquito net."

I smiled to myself in triumph. "Thank you. Enjoy yourself."

"You know, you're right. I probably will. What do we tell the others?"

Dane and Noah weren't going to be brought in on this little scheme. Not until it was already over. "I'll convince them you're on vacation," I said.

Alex snorted. "Good luck with that, but that's your problem. I'm off to buy some SPF 50."

After I hung up, I had a brief moment of second thoughts. Samantha likely wouldn't approve of what I was doing. Not that she had any affection for the Egerton brothers, but she wasn't the type of person to take out a long, protracted, expensive revenge.

I was.

I'd told her I wasn't a very good person.

Besides, it didn't matter. Tomorrow, we weren't going to be ourselves anyway.

I picked up my phone and texted her. *Jacques Bar, 10:20 p.m.*

I had told her to wait for my instructions, and here they were. Bossy and a little imperious. I'd made the time puzzlingly specific in order to throw her off her game.

There was an agonizing minute in which I got no response, and then another. Finally, a single word came through by text:

Yes

I smiled and tossed my phone down. The game was on.

NINETEEN

Samantha

JACQUES BAR, 10:20 *p.m.*

I swiped the wand of mascara over my lashes, leaning close to the mirror. When I was finished I stood straight and studied the finished product.

My dress was black, knee length, sleeveless, fitted. It was snug in the bodice with a low, square neckline, the suggestion of corset-like curves at my waist. There was a slit three inches up my left thigh and the whole thing fit me like a glove. It was a dress that cost more than even my considerable salary allowed, but today I had bought it anyway.

I'd accessorized it with a silver necklace, silver bracelets, and black heeled mules. I'd bought an expensive sapphire ring, and I put it on the third finger of my right hand. I had my hair up in the back, with large pieces drifting down in front and framing my face. Dark, smoky liner around my eyes. Understated gloss on my lips.

I never looked like this. I could dress properly, and I usually did, but this... this was entirely different. The dress, the hair, the ring—all of it was classy, yet somehow it was showy at the same time. The sort of look that said *I'm a very rich woman, so rich I buy what I want.* And although I had a good job now, I had come from very humble beginnings, so that woman was not me.

My smoke-lined eyes kept drawing my attention in the mirror. I was a professional, and though I never went out in public without makeup, I always kept it understated. Years of working for CEOs had taught me never to give anyone in the office the wrong impression. Too-short skirts gave the wrong impression, as did too-low tops and too-high heels. And fuck-me eye makeup *definitely* gave the wrong impression. So I never wore it.

But I was wearing it tonight. I was wearing all of it. And I felt... perfect. Free.

I flipped off the bathroom light and picked up my small purse. At the door of my condo, I paused for just the briefest second as the doubts came in.

He's not going to be there.

He was joking.

He was horny and not serious.

He doesn't think like you do, doesn't want you the same way you want him.

He's going to stand you up. On Monday it will be awkward, he'll apologize, and both of you will pretend it never happened.

It was a test, just to see if you would do it. A dare, that's all.

This isn't going to work.

And most of all, again: *He's not going to be there.*

The Jacques was one of the classiest and most expensive bars in the city, attached to a five-star hotel on the Upper East Side called the Lowell. I had never been there. To be stood up at the Jacques, after I'd spent a good percentage of my paycheck, would be embarrassing. Humiliating, even.

But the game was already in motion. If Aidan Winters—or whoever he was tonight—was going to stand me up, I would find out in the next twenty minutes. Taking a breath, I left my place and locked the door behind me.

It was ten o'clock p.m.

IT WAS A BEAUTIFUL BAR. It was small enough to be intimate, large enough that couples could sit at the tables and talk without being overheard. The maitre d' gave me a nod and a smile as I entered and told him I was going to have a drink at the bar. At first I thought he must recognize me from somewhere, but then I realized it was the dress. In the dress I looked like I belonged here.

There was only one available seat at the bar. I let my eyes sweep once across the backs of the other customers—he wasn't here—and then I sat, silently admiring the dark brown and gold finishes, the subtle lights, the impeccable white jacket and black tie of the bartender. When he asked what I wanted, I ordered a martini. When he gave it to me I sipped it, letting the place soothe my excited nerves.

It was understated, but the other patrons here were rich. I worked for rich people, and I knew them when I saw them. I also knew people who wore their wealth like a well-worn old coat, one they were comfortable in and never took off. Somewhere in their logical minds, these people knew that wearing a three-thousand-dollar blouse wasn't real life for most people, but deep down it didn't compute. It was real for them, and that was all that mattered.

They weren't obnoxious, and they didn't show off. Couples, most of them older, sat talking quietly, and a couple groups of suited men had quiet, intense conversations. Probably deciding the financial fate of the world as they sipped whiskey. Or maybe they were just talking about golf.

No one looked twice at me. No one told me I didn't belong, that it would be best if I left. Even the bartender, who likely knew most of these people by name, didn't give me the side-eye. I had spent years studying, and as a result I played my part well.

But it was ten twenty-five, and I was still alone. Then ten twenty-seven. Ten twenty-nine.

The sixtyish couple sitting next to me at the bar paid their tab, got up, and left. A man slid into the open seat beside me. And just like that, the hairs on the back of my neck stood up. Because I knew that scent. I knew that man.

"Bourbon," he said to the bartender, his voice in that one word going down my spine.

My heart did a little spin of triumph, but I tamped it down and tried to get into character. I could do this. I was almost completely in control when I let myself glance at him, just once, the way I would glance at a stranger. I had to look away in shock.

Aidan wasn't wearing black. He was wearing a dark blue four-button suit with a white shirt and a tie of lighter blue. The top button of his shirt was undone and his tie was loosened an inch, as if he were unwinding from work. He was clean-shaven and his dark hair was mussed. A gold watch I had never seen before glinted on his wrist. I had never seen my boss wear anything but black, and the effect was startling, as if he were a different man.

That was the idea. I had to think of him as a stranger. The blue suit made it easy, just as I hoped my dress and makeup made it easier for him. I smiled privately to myself as I sipped my martini. For once, I was wearing black and he wasn't. The switch was delicious.

Then I stopped thinking of him as Aidan at all.

In the corner of my vision, a beautiful masculine hand reached out and lay casually on the bar. "Magazine editor," the voice next to me said.

I gave him another brief glance. "I'm sorry?"

He was looking at me, his dark eyes speculative. With his other hand, he touched his fingertips to his crystal bourbon glass. "I'm trying to guess what you do," he said. "Hotelier. No, that's not right. Head of marketing. Director of a fashion line."

I couldn't help it; I was a little amused. "Is this a pickup line?"

"I don't use lines," he said. "I just talk. What's your name?"

"You don't use lines because you don't pick up women, or because you don't need lines to pick up women?"

"That's too complicated a question. Here's a simple one. What's your name?"

Oh, he's good. The thought gave me a thrill, like I was going over the first hill in a roller coaster ride. I was in the hands of a master. "Sarah," I said.

His eyelid didn't even twitch. Not a ghost of an admission of the lie crossed his expression. "Nice to meet you, Sarah," he said. "I'm John."

There was the briefest pause between us, an acknowledgment that we were going downhill on the roller coaster together. The momentum was starting. We weren't Samantha and Aidan, we were Sarah and John. We were both in this. We were doing it.

I was more turned on than I could remember being in years.

I held out my hand, partly because that was something Sarah would do, and partly because I felt the overwhelming need to touch him. He raised a brow and shook my hand in greeting. His touch was as warm and strong as I remembered. I recalled that touch against the back of my neck, and I felt the shiver of it all the way down to my lower back. Between my legs. He could do that to me with just a handshake.

Still, I turned back to my martini and took a sip. "I'm not any of those things you guessed," I said. "Sorry."

"Okay, then. Tell me what you do."

I licked a drop of alcohol off my glossed lip, still looking ahead. "I run a finance company."

"You're the president?"

"The CEO."

I'd thought of that in advance. I didn't know everything about who Sarah was—I'd improvise—but that much I knew. After so many years of working for them, tonight I was a CEO.

"That's interesting," Aidan—John—said. "By the laws of the jungle, you and I should be oil and water."

"Why?"

"Because I deal in art for a living, while you deal in cold-blooded money."

That made my thoughts turn. Aidan had chosen to be an art dealer tonight. I wondered why. "If you mean that you buy and sell art, then you definitely deal in cold-blooded money," I said.

He smiled at me. I felt that smile deep in my belly, felt it thrum between my legs and in my nipples. "I deal in beauty," he said. "I deal in passion and raw emotion." He lifted his bourbon glass and looked at it in the golden light of the bar. "The money just appears. Though I'm not complaining."

My throat was dry, watching him. "You make enough of it to have a drink here."

"Because I'm staying here." He took a sip.

He was staying here? At the Lowell? The place was a thousand dollars a night. And then a thrill of excitement shivered up my back. He had a room, just upstairs. Minutes away.

I took another sip of martini, feeling it burn down my throat. I turned to find him looking at me, his dark eyes fixed on me. Our gazes held. I couldn't look away.

"What are you doing here, Sarah?" he asked, his voice low.

You. I came here for you. The words rose to my lips, but I didn't say them. Instead I said, "I've had a hard week. I'm tired of making decisions. I want a drink, and I want to stop thinking, and I don't want to sleep alone."

There it was. The words I would never say to a stranger I'd just met in a bar. But I could say them to this particular stranger. This stranger, and no one else.

I kept my gaze on him, reading his reaction, because I knew how to read every line of his face. His dark eyes didn't even flinch.

"So don't," he said.

I wanted him. If there was a way to hide that, I didn't know what it was. I wanted to taste him and to touch him. I didn't care if he was picking me up in a bar for a one-night stand. I wanted him any way I could get him, for as long as I could have him. Wanting him had brought me this far, doing something I'd never imagined doing. And now it was driving me crazy.

John the art dealer put his drink down. He reached into his pocket and put a few bills on the bar. Then, thank God, he stood, turning to look at me.

"Let's go," he said.

TWENTY

Samantha

IT WAS A LOVELY HOTEL, I was sure. I didn't pay attention.

As Sarah, I followed John to the elevator. My heels clicked on the marble floor. I could feel the pulse beating in my throat.

We had the elevator to ourselves. As the doors closed, John swiped his card and pressed the button. Then he turned, cupped a hand to the back of my head, and kissed me.

He tasted like man. Like bourbon. Like pleasure. *Finally. Finally.* I slid my hands under his jacket and let him open my mouth. Incredibly, with the desire that was drenching both of us, he teased me, running his tongue along the inside of my lip, letting his teeth scrape my skin. His fingers pushed into my hair, his thumbs pressing just below my ears, the heat of his body radiating to mine. I ran my hands down his chest, his perfect stomach. God, he was so gorgeous.

He broke away, not moving far from my mouth. "You didn't say yes," he said.

I moved my hand further down, slid my fingers beneath his belt. "Yes," I said.

His body tensed under my touch, his muscles flexing in surprise. I paused my hand. "You're very forward," he said.

Sarah wouldn't give a damn about that. "Do you object?"

In answer he leaned down and kissed the side of my neck, letting his teeth scrape the sensitive skin. I let out a breath and my eyes closed in bliss. Every nerve ending in my body was on fire.

"I think I can make you a little more obedient," he said in my ear.

Before I could answer, the bell pinged and the elevator doors opened. John pulled my hand from under his belt and led me down the hall.

I followed him. The longer I did this, the more I was Sarah. The man leading me into his hotel room wasn't my boss, he was a stranger I'd just met an hour ago. I was a woman who spoke her desires and got what she wanted, and what I wanted was sex for one night with the man before me. I didn't know this stranger's last name, and it didn't matter. I was going to have him anyway.

He didn't turn the lights on in the room. He closed the door behind me and pulled me into another kiss, this one deeper. I kissed him back as I tugged his tie out of its knot.

He broke the kiss as I dropped the tie on the floor and pushed his jacket off his shoulders. "That forwardness again," he said in the dim light, amused.

I dropped the jacket alongside the tie. "I'm used to getting what I want." The words felt good to say.

"And what do you want?" he asked.

I ran my hands over his shoulders through the thin fabric of his dress shirt. I traced their lines with my palms, then started on his buttons. "I told you, I want to stop thinking for a while." The words were the truth, I realized even as I said them. "To think about nothing. To feel." I looked at his gorgeous face in the shadows. "What do you want?"

He put a hand to my waist and pulled me to him, dropping his mouth to my neck. I could feel the hard muscles of his body against me, his chest against the fabric on my breasts. "I think you'll find my wants are very simple," he said against my skin. "Turn around."

I obeyed. His deft hands found my zipper and unzipped my dress, letting it pool to the floor at my feet. I sighed. My oversensitized skin had felt constrained by the tight fabric.

Now I was in my black bra, my panties, and my heels. John stepped up behind me, ran a strong hand from the back of my neck down my spine. "Walk to the bedroom," he said.

I didn't even think of disobeying. I walked across the room to the lush bedroom, where the bed was piled high with luxurious pillows. The blinds on the window were partly open, and the winking lights of New York were the only illumination in the room. There was just us, high above the city in the dark.

I walked to the edge of the bed and he stopped me, his hand on the back of my neck again. It was commanding, though it wasn't rough. I leaned into his touch without thinking and closed my eyes.

He stepped up behind me and put his palms on my stomach. I could feel the fabric of his thighs against my ass, his shirt against my back. His warm body beneath the layer of fabric. His palms moved up my body until they cupped my breasts through the thin lace fabric of my bra.

I gasped and leaned my weight back, my head resting on his shoulder. My breasts weren't overly big and his hands engulfed them easily, stroking and gently squeezing. I felt every movement between my legs.

Again he dropped his mouth to my skin. "I know what you want," he said as one hand moved down my belly, beneath my panties, and his fingers slid into my pussy.

I moaned, not quietly, my head still resting back against his shoulder. I wasn't thinking now. I pushed my hips up into his hand.

He was touching me. This stranger, this man I didn't know, was stroking me, and I was letting him. He could feel how wet I was, feel how desperate I was. The thought just made me hotter.

"You want someone to touch you," John said, his fingers moving in a slow, sure rhythm. "You want someone to make you feel good. No names, no attachments, no expectations. Just pleasure. That's what I want, too."

His fingers moved down to my entrance, then up to my clit, sure and easy. I squirmed and closed my eyes. Everything in the world vanished but his hand, his voice, the feeling of his body against my back. This was already better than anything I'd ever experienced, and he wasn't even fucking me. Any inhibitions I had were vanishing under the stroke of his fingers.

His voice lowered to a growl against my skin. "You want to be pleased," he said, his hand still moving. "You want to be told what to do and pleasured at the same time. You don't want an amateur. That wouldn't be nearly enough for you. You want a man who knows what the fuck he's doing."

The orgasm shivered through me, starting somewhere behind my knees, on the insides of my thighs, then shaking my whole body. Sounds I didn't recognize came out of my mouth, and I would have lost my balance if I hadn't been leaning against him, if he didn't have me in his grip. I kept my eyes closed, and he held me through every aftershock until I started to come down.

His fingers hooked beneath the elastic at my hips and he pulled my panties down, letting them drop to the floor. "Put your hands on the bed," he said, his voice hoarse.

I did. I leaned forward and did as he said, and now I was in an incredibly vulnerable position, naked and exposed to him, unable to see him. My heart was racing, competing with the post-orgasm bliss running through my body. I heard the click of his belt, the soft sound of a zipper. Then the crinkle of a condom package.

He leaned over me, and I felt fabric against my back; he still had his shirt on. "I wanted to do this the first second I saw you," he said, and pushed into me.

I closed my eyes again, a breath escaping my throat. Good. It felt *so good*. He made a low sound that was tightly wound, yet mirrored my own pleasure, and then he moved out, then in again.

I curled my hands in the bedspread as we found a rhythm. He was in perfect command as he pushed deep into me, then deeper again, yet the ragged sound of his breath told me he was as consumed as I was. His strong hands dug into my hips as he dropped his mouth to my ear. "You feel fucking incredible," he said.

I shivered at his words, a tremor of pleasure that shook my whole body. He must have felt it, because his movements grew sharper, his breath more harsh. I rode the waves until he finally stilled, letting out another harsh breath as he came.

There was a second of silence, both of us catching our breath. Then he braced a hand on the bed and stood, pulling out of me. I heard him walk to the bathroom and close the door.

I turned and sat on the bed, my hands nearly shaking. For the first time tonight, doubt washed over me like a bucket of cold water. I felt incredible, my body and brain still singing with pleasure. But what happened now? Was the game over, or did we keep playing? Was I expected to leave?

We'd set no rules, no plan. Until a few minutes ago, it had been thrilling. Now I wondered if I was supposed to take my cue, get dressed, and walk out without a word.

My fantasy, of course, had never included this particular part of the scene. No one's fantasy did—the aftermath, the decision whether or not to make eye contact, whether or not to talk, whether one or both of us was supposed to sleep, was not fantasy material. Like everyone else, I ended my fantasies at the orgasm and didn't think any further. And now I didn't know what to do.

In the bathroom, the water ran. He'd come out a minute from now, still dressed, and find me sitting on the edge of the bed, wearing only my bra and my heels. It was going to be strange. Reluctantly, I leaned down and picked up my panties from the floor, untangling them so I could put them back on.

The bathroom door opened, and Aidan walked out. No, John. Was I still supposed to think of him as John?

The top buttons of his shirt were undone, his hair slightly disheveled. Otherwise he was dressed, as if all he had to do was slip on his tie and his jacket and go back down to the bar. His dark gaze moved over me, then dropped to my hands, which held my panties.

"What are you doing?" he asked.

Was that surprise in his voice? I couldn't tell. I went for the obvious answer. "I'm putting these on."

His gaze came back up to my face. "I wouldn't do that if I were you, Sarah," he said. "We aren't even close to finished."

TWENTY-ONE

Aidan

IF I WAS BEING PAINFULLY honest—and at this point, I had no choice—I went into the bathroom mostly to collect myself. To gather my wits and get myself together. To take a breath and be Aidan again.

Except I wasn't Aidan. Or was I? We hadn't planned this far —*I* hadn't planned this far. I'd planned the seduction, but like an idiot I hadn't thought about what would come afterward.

The seduction itself had nearly pulled me to pieces.

I'd never had an experience like that with any woman. Samantha, playing Sarah, was fucking amazing. She was confident and sexy, raw and vulnerable. She played a game of deception, while underneath I could sense all of her exposed nerves. The combination was brilliant, erotic, and so explosive I'd nearly broken character a dozen times. It had taken every ounce of self-control I had not to throw the whole game away.

But I hadn't. Because she liked the game, and so did I. The question was, now that we had both come and she was naked on my bed, were we still playing it?

Part of me wanted to go out there as Aidan and take her in my arms. Ask how she was feeling, if she was still okay. Talk to her about what we'd just done and how we'd done it.

But even as I cleaned up, then ran a hand through my hair as I looked in the mirror, I knew that would be the wrong move. There was a reason for this game—a reason beyond our own pleasure, that was. It was the only way to keep our other relationship, our work relationship, alive.

In short, if I ended the game now, on Monday Samantha would quit. And that was unthinkable.

So, John the art dealer it was.

I walked back out of the bathroom to see Sarah—I had to think of her as Sarah—sitting on the edge of the bed, naked except for her bra and her shoes. Her hair was only slightly mussed, her makeup—that black eye makeup, so bold and so unlike her—still in place. Her knees were pressed together, a decorous pose for a woman so naked, and she was holding her black panties in her hand.

As if she was leaving.

That was when I realized—Sarah leaving my room after a quick fuck was definitely *not* part of the game.

"What are you doing?" I asked her.

She looked up at me. In that look, I knew that she was as lost as I was, that she didn't know how the game went now either. For some reason that gave me confidence. She was looking for me to take the lead, so I would.

"I'm putting these on," she said, her voice neutral. Waiting for me to give her a signal.

"I wouldn't do that if I were you, Sarah," I said. "We aren't even close to finished."

There it was: my signal. If she wanted to end the game, all she had to do was put her clothes on and walk out. I wouldn't stop her.

There was the briefest flicker in her eyes, which gave me satisfaction. Then she blinked. "You're awfully confident that I'll want another round," she said.

I smiled at her. I raised my hands and began unbuttoning my shirt. "You loved it."

"You were adequate." But her expression gave her away, her hungry eyes, as they followed every move of my fingers, taking in my skin as I unbuttoned the shirt.

"I don't see you leaving." I pulled the shirt off and dropped it, started on my belt. "In fact, I don't even see you putting those panties on. So drop them."

Her eyes moved down me. "I'll do it if you drop your pants first, John."

Did she put the slightest emphasis on that last word? Maybe. I didn't care. I was John now, the art dealer who had started his evening having a lonely drink at a bar and ended it unexpectedly lucky. John was impulsive, a man who didn't make many plans but always followed a streak of luck if he found one.

In short, he was the opposite of me. He wasn't the icy cold Man in Black, who never made a move without thinking it through. No, John improvised. He took chances on pieces of art that spoke to him. He took chances on beautiful women in bars who were far, far out of his league. As a result, what had started out as yet another lonely night was turning into one of the best nights of his life.

This woman, Sarah the CEO, was a challenge. John knew he had to up his game to please her, even for just one night. She was used to being disappointed, and he wasn't planning on disappointing her.

Besides, he really, really wanted to fuck her again.

I kicked off my shoes and socks, then dropped my pants. Pushed off my boxer briefs and kicked them away, too.

Her eyes were wide and dark as she took me in, head to toe. For once she didn't have anything smart to say.

I took a step toward her. "Your turn," I said. I was already half hard again, which wasn't a surprise, because the hottest woman I'd ever seen was sitting on this bed, her round, pert breasts tucked behind a scrap of lace bra and no other clothes on. Just the thought of that perfect, bare ass against the bedsheets made heat travel down my spine. Her gaze fixed on my cock and stayed there.

It was flattering, but I was impatient. I stepped close and took the panties from her hand. "First, these," I said, dropping them. "Then these." I lifted one of her ankles and pulled off one high heel, then the other.

I put a finger under her chin and tilted her face up so she was looking me in the eyes again. "Adequate?" I asked her.

"Um," she said, a soft, utterly turned-on sound, and I pressed my advantage. I kissed her, taking her mouth, letting my tongue slide in. She groaned softly and sucked on me, as if she'd been waiting for this and nothing else. My cock got harder. Still kissing her, I reached behind her and unclasped her bra.

Her hands dragged down my chest, my stomach. I cupped her breasts gently, running my thumbs over her nipples. "I've been waiting to see these," I said. In truth, I'd been waiting to see them for three months, not just tonight. But I hoped she didn't see through me.

She stopped touching me—it was almost painful—and lifted her hands behind her head. She pulled the pins from her hair, letting it fall past her shoulders. Then she moved back on the bed and lay down, her hair falling against the bedspread, her gaze still on me, serious and intent.

We'd moved past a quick fuck in a hotel room, but I didn't

care. This was what I wanted—what I had wanted for a long time. This woman, naked on a bed, relaxed and ready for me. Trusting me. I kissed my way up her ribcage, her breasts. Her shoulder and the dip of her clavicle. I nibbled her neck, feeling her go warm and soft beneath me, listening to her breath come faster.

Her hands ran through my hair. "I'm never going to see you again, am I?" she asked.

"Never," I said, which was easy because it was a fucking lie.

"This is just tonight."

I sucked her earlobe. "Yes." Another fucking lie, if I had any say in it.

Her voice was hoarse with desire as she said, "Good, because that's what I want."

I settled my hips between her legs, pressing my now-hard cock against her. "I think I've made it clear that I know exactly what you want."

"Oh," she said, and by instinct I knew that wasn't a Sarah sound. That was a Samantha sound. It made my cock throb harder against her skin. I kissed her again.

Eventually we parted long enough for me to find a condom in the stash I'd put here earlier. I put it on and rolled back over her. I braced myself with one hand, and with the other I grasped both of her wrists, squeezing them together as I pushed her hands above her head. There was no harshness to it, and she could easily escape, but it was a signal that I was taking control.

"Oh, that's nice," she said as I put her in position. "I mean, I think—oh, *God*."

I slid into her in one smooth thrust, angled just right, as far as I could go. The first round had taken the edge off, and now we could take our time. I tried to hold off my own orgasm and do it right.

She was so perfect beneath me, naked, her hair spread, her

arms pinned above her head. "Relax," I told her as I moved. "I'm going to make you come."

She bit her lip. "I think you are," she said, her voice a whisper. "I think you are."

In that moment, she was mine. Completely. Later, we'd dress and I'd go home alone. Later, I'd sit alone in my penthouse, unable to sleep. But right now, I was the man who completely possessed this woman. The man who got to see her like this, feel her. The man who got to listen to the perfect sounds she made when she came.

I didn't care that our time would be up.

Right now, this was the only man I wanted to be.

TWENTY-TWO

Samantha

AND THEN... Monday morning came.

It was warm and sunny, the sky high above the skyscrapers a beautiful blue. Spring was warming New York. I dressed at six as usual, eating breakfast in my kitchen and checking my boss's schedule on my phone.

My boss, Aidan Winters. Who I definitely had not fucked on Saturday night.

Oh, God.

You can do this, Samantha.

In my work clothes and my regular makeup, I looked nothing like Sarah, the woman who had picked up a stranger in a bar. The man she had hooked up with was a beautiful specimen in a dark blue suit, not New York's infamous Man in Black.

I scrolled through Aidan's schedule for today. He was scheduled to be at the Monday meeting, which was a company-wide check-in to set up the week. Since Tower had only twenty employees in the New York office, it was easy to have meetings that included everyone. Sometimes Aidan attended them and sometimes he didn't. Today he was going to be there.

He had more meetings in the afternoon: with Finance, with Legal. After staying away from the office for weeks to avoid me, now he was going to be there all day. It was probably on purpose, because everything Aidan did was on purpose. *Let's see if we can get along,* this schedule said. *I'm willing to try if you are.*

There was one way to find out. I finished my breakfast and went to work.

I GOT to the office at eight and did my usual routine. I opened Aidan's office and booted up his MacBook. I prepped the meeting room for the Monday meeting. I went through Aidan's email, sorting the urgent from the not-so-urgent and the garbage. I picked up the firm's mail from the receptionist at the front desk and sorted through the things that Aidan would need to see.

At eight forty-five, I heard his voice in the open office, talking to the receptionist. As if I had a radar attached to me, I heard his footsteps as he walked into his office and sat at his desk.

The moment of truth. I picked up papers from my own desk and walked—briskly, normally—to his office door.

Aidan was behind his desk, dressed in his usual black. He was clean-shaven, his hair combed neatly back from his forehead, his dark eyes intent as he read something on his MacBook screen. He looked up at me, and his expression gave nothing away. "Good morning, Samantha."

"Morning," I said. I stepped into the office and put a paper on his desk. "This is the itinerary for the Monday meeting. Oscar is sick today, so he's going to phone in."

"Did the signed contracts get sent to Wells and Vane?"

"I couriered them first thing. I'll get a call when the receptionist signs for them."

"They have to be there by ten."

"They will be."

It was a normal conversation. We'd had a dozen Monday morning conversations just like it. And what I felt as we talked was pure, unmixed relief. With the strangeness of Chicago and the weeks afterward, I'd missed Aidan, my boss. I'd missed my job, which I genuinely liked. I'd missed feeling normal.

We were normal again, thanks to the game.

Well, almost normal. When he handed me papers, the sight of his hand reminded me of the moment when it was inside my black panties, making me come as he said dirty things in my ear. And I definitely, definitely wasn't thinking about him deep inside me, saying *I'm going to make you come.* Which he had.

Those things had happened to different people. I had a staff meeting to arrange.

We had finished our business conversation, and Aidan had drunk most of his first coffee of the day. I was turning to leave his office when he said, "Oh, Samantha, there's one more thing."

"Yes?" I turned back.

"I have some dry cleaning I need to have picked up this afternoon. Do you mind doing it for me?"

Never, not once, had Aidan made me pick up his dry cleaning. He'd always treated that job as beneath me. For a second I was angry, and then I remembered Aidan never did anything unless it was on purpose.

He was up to something.

His expression gave nothing away, so I said, "Picking up dry cleaning isn't really in my job description, Aidan. Maybe you should get an intern."

He leaned back in his chair. "I don't trust an intern with the codes to my penthouse, Samantha. I only trust you."

His penthouse. I'd never been there, though I knew he lived on the Upper East Side. "You need your dry cleaning dropped off at your penthouse?"

"I would appreciate it." He paused, then added, "Just this once. And I'm asking nicely."

We had a momentary standoff. I gave in, not because he was my boss, but because I wanted to know what the game was. "Just this once," I said.

He pulled a set of keys out and slid them across the desk to me. "I'll text you the address and the entry codes," he said. "And I'll tell the concierge you're there with my permission. You can go anytime."

AIDAN'S BUILDING was at Third Ave and 83rd Street, a low-rise red brick building with immaculate wrought iron railings. The noise of Manhattan was hushed here, as if this were a different city. My own Hell's Kitchen apartment—which was far from cheap—seemed a long way away. The only sounds were a few car honks a few blocks away and the barking of a dog.

I got out of the taxi, the dry cleaning bag with Aidan's clothes in it over my arm. The doorman let me in with a smile and a nod; he was expecting me. The foyer was clean white marble, the elevator to the sixth floor classic with a wrought-iron door. The entire building was as hushed as a library.

The elevator doors opened to the penthouse suite, and I typed in Aidan's code. The door clicked and I opened it.

Aidan's apartment was beautiful, a huge open-concept space with a bathroom and bedroom on one side. The main room held a dark gray sofa, square and masculine, with a matching dark coffee table. The kitchen had marble counters and gleaming steel appliances. A bank of windows overlooked 83rd Street, facing north. Next to the windows was a glass-topped desk with a computer on it and stacks of papers on it.

I stood looking around, curious. I'd seen plenty of my former bosses' apartments when I dropped off mail, fed pets, or picked up forgotten jackets or cell phones. I was no stranger to luxurious places to live. In all of those cases, I'd never had the urge to snoop, which was why I was so good at my job. I may have had their security codes, but my bosses' private business was just that —private.

Still, none of my previous bosses had been Aidan Winters.

I shouldn't look around too closely. Then again, he'd invited me here, hadn't he?

The dry cleaning was heavy over my arm, so I walked to the bedroom. It was masculine in here, too, the king-sized bed swathed in a navy comforter, a dark wood nightstand and matching dresser along one wall. The bed was made, but hastily, the blankets pulled up and left slightly mussed. He didn't have a maid service, then, or at least not one that had been here today. I looked away from the bed, trying not to picture Aidan's long body, possibly naked, sprawled out on it.

His closet was big and contained a lot of black clothes, as expected. But as I hung the dry cleaning bag I also saw other colors. There were casual pants and button-downs, and a stack of sweaters on the top shelf. The suit I'd seen on him Saturday night was in there. The closet smelled like Aidan, a scent I'd become closely acquainted with. I ran my fingertips over one of the shirts, remembering what he had tasted like when he kissed me in the elevator of the Lowell hotel.

Get it together, Samantha.

I backed out of the closet and closed the door. I looked around, wondering why Aidan had sent me here. Was it just to have me in his private space, to know that I had been there? Or was there another reason? He wasn't trying to impress me with his expensive penthouse—he wasn't the type, and he must know I wouldn't be impressed anyway. There was something here he wanted me to see.

When I came back out into the main room, I spotted it. An envelope on the kitchen counter. I picked it up and took out the piece of paper inside.

It was a ticket to an exclusive art gallery showing. The gallery was in SoHo, the artist was obscure but trendy, and tickets were limited. The show was this Saturday night.

I ran my finger over the edge of the invitation, thinking. This was obviously an invitation to continue the game. The question was, did I want to continue it?

Last Saturday had been incredible. I'd discovered aspects of myself I never knew I had. I wanted that again.

But today he'd made me pick up his dry cleaning.

I couldn't make things too easy for him. I had to make him suffer a little. I could make him wonder what I was going to do next instead of assuming he owned me.

I put the ticket in my purse. Then I walked back into Aidan's bedroom. Standing next to his bed, I lifted my skirt and slid off my panties. They were a pair of my favorites—slate gray, slim cut, soft as my own skin. They undoubtedly smelled like me. I put them on Aidan's pillow.

Then I left the apartment, locking it behind me.

TWENTY-THREE

Aidan

IT WAS A HELLISH WEEK. I had no idea time could go so slow. Saturday seemed to be years away.

Samantha had given me not a flicker of a signal when she came back to the office on Monday afternoon. I'd come home to find the ticket gone from my kitchen counter and her panties left on my pillow. I'd groaned aloud, alone in my bedroom, at the thought that she'd spent the afternoon at work bare beneath her skirt and *I hadn't fucking known.* It was like she was born to torture me.

I'd been tempted to take a shower and jerk off, thinking about it. But I didn't. She was teasing me. I'd have some self-control.

So on Tuesday I went to the office all business. I went to meetings, reviewed reports, and met with Samantha about my schedule. Looking at us, no one in the office would guess that I'd had her bent over a hotel room bed, her hands in the sheets, her legs spread for me. No one would know that I knew what color her nipples were, knew what her skin tasted like, knew exactly what sound she made when she came. We were the same boss and assistant we'd always been. And that made the game more exciting to play.

Finally, on Friday afternoon—a thousand years later—I went over a few end-of-week notes with Samantha in my office. I watched her sitting in the chair across from my desk, her legs crossed and her head angled down as she wrote a note on her notepad, and I said, "Do you have any plans for the weekend?"

She didn't look up; she kept writing. But a smile touched the corner of her mouth. Of course it did—she'd just won a victory. I hadn't meant to cave in and ask her, but the words had just come out. Damn her.

She took her time answering, finishing her note first before looking up. "I'm not sure," she said. "I haven't decided."

I met her gaze. "So, a quiet weekend at home, then."

She shrugged, as if I hadn't given her a ticket to SoHo's most exclusive art show. "Possibly," she said with believable casualness. "Possibly not."

I nodded. "I hear there are some very good shows on Netflix right now. You know, if you're spending the weekend alone on the couch."

A muscle in her cheek twitched in annoyance. "Is that so?"

"Yes. Maybe you should join a meetup group. Try to make friends if you're lonely."

"You're full of advice today." She put her pen down. "It's very generous of you."

My pulse started to beat a little bit faster. "I'm just trying to be helpful. You live in New York, you know. If you want to find something to do on the weekend, there's plenty happening."

"I see." Was that a flush on her cheeks? "And what exactly are your exciting plans?"

I shrugged. "You know my schedule is empty. I always find something to do. There's an art exhibit in SoHo I'll probably attend."

"Because you're an art fan," she said. It wasn't a question.

"Sometimes, yes. I find looking at art a pleasant way to spend a Saturday night."

"And you plan to attend by yourself."

"If you believe the tabloids, yes."

Samantha narrowed her eyes, and I fought off a smile. Fuck, this was fun. "Well," she said finally, "I hope that you have a nice time, whatever you decide." She stood and picked up her notebook.

"You, too," I said. "Goodbye, Samantha. See you Monday."

"Hm," she said noncommittally, walking out of the office and closing the door behind her.

This was definitely going to be good.

We were going to play the game again.

TWENTY-FOUR

Samantha

THE AIR on Saturday night was warm and thick, slathered like honey. I stood in front of my mirrored closet and looked myself over, assessing the effect.

A button-front shirtdress from Target, navy blue with small white flowers. Bare legs, white flat sandals. Very little makeup, my hair tied in a ponytail at the back of my neck. A gray cardigan over my shoulders. Once again, I looked nothing like my usual self. Tonight I was an art student who had scored a ticket to an edgy art show from her roommate, who had come down with the flu.

In real life, I had gone to college for exactly one year, taking business courses before Emma hired me straight into Executive Ranks to be an executive assistant. I hadn't made lifelong college friends, and I'd only had one year of partying and dating college guys. I certainly had never been an art student, spending her time studying something that was pretty much proven never to make money. I had never been a girl to follow my passion no matter what the cost.

So tonight, I would be that girl.

And tonight, that girl would meet a man.

I wondered who he would be tonight. Would he be an art dealer again? It made sense, yet I didn't think Aidan would use the same identity again. That wasn't how the game worked. If he was John the art dealer, then he wasn't a stranger.

Which meant I was on the lookout for someone else. How would he dress? How would he look? Would he be rich or poor? I already felt the excitement starting between my legs, beneath my thin cotton panties. I'd considered leaving them off, but decided that Rachel the art student would never go to a gallery showing without panties.

There was something to be said for staying in character.

I looked at my bed, where the ticket Aidan had left me was sitting. *Last chance to back out, Samantha. Sit on the couch and watch Netflix, just like he said.*

It was probably the wisest course of action, but there was no chance.

I took the ticket, put it in my purse, and left for SoHo.

BY ELEVEN THIRTY, I had been through the entire exhibit and looked at all of the art. I had eaten a couple of the appetizers and drunk two glasses of champagne. Even though this was an exclusive exhibit, I didn't look out of place here in my Target dress. The art lovers here were all types—eccentric artists, hipster critics, queer and gender-fluid people, a woman with a long black cigarette holder, a man wearing a rainbow cloak and a cloud-of-weed smell. It was pure New York. The art was interesting, the people even more so, and I enjoyed myself.

The problem was that Aidan wasn't here.

There was no way I had misunderstood—he had definitely left me that ticket on the counter in his penthouse. And he had grilled me thoroughly on Friday, trying to dig out of me whether I was coming or not. I had played it cagey, but now I started to wonder if I had done it too well. Had I convinced Aidan that I wasn't coming?

The thought was so disappointing it was hard to face. The game Aidan and I played had gone flawlessly so far; we had followed it perfectly without having to discuss it after that first time. It was like we were reading each other's minds. I'd thought he'd understood on Friday that I was playing the opening round of the game by keeping him guessing. I hadn't thought he would take it as a serious rejection.

Maybe he wasn't sure I'd enjoyed the first round, I thought as I put down my empty glass and wound my cardigan around my shoulders, giving up at last. It was hard to fathom, because when a woman leaves her panties on a man's pillow, she's giving him a pretty clear message about what she wants. Which left the option that maybe *he* hadn't enjoyed himself as much as I thought he did. Maybe it was Aidan who was having second thoughts.

But if he wasn't enjoying the game, then why had he left me the ticket?

My thoughts went round and round, and I was so caught up in them that the rain took me by surprise. When I stepped out of the gallery it was pouring as if the skies had opened. And damn it, I needed a cab.

I pulled up the collar of my cardigan and stepped onto the sidewalk. Immediately my feet were soaked in their sandals, the water squishing unpleasantly beneath my feet. I darted to the curb and looked hopelessly into traffic, putting my arm up in case some cab I couldn't see would take pity on me. Meanwhile the rain got my cardigan wet and pelted down the front of my dress.

One cab passed me, and then another. The third added insult to injury by splashing a wave of dirty street water over the front of my dress. In the meantime I stood there getting wetter and wetter, my hair soaked to my head, my cardigan getting heavy with water.

This night just kept getting better.

I lowered my arm long enough to grab the hem of my cardigan and use it to mop my face. It was a useless effort, but I did my best. When I dropped the wet wool I realized it wasn't raining on me anymore. Someone was standing over me with an umbrella.

"You look like you need help," a familiar voice said.

I turned to look at him. He was wearing black pants, a dark gray dress shirt open at the throat. His sleeves were rolled to the elbow and he wore no jacket. He hadn't shaved this morning, and his jaw was shadowed with just the perfect shade of dark stubble. His hair was mussed and damp with rain, his dark eyes fixed on me. The entire effect was so gorgeous, and he was so close, that my knees went weak.

I took a deep breath, inhaled him. Then I remembered I was angry.

He'd stood me up and left me to hail a cab in the rain. Who the hell did he think he was?

"I'm fine, thank you," I said coldly.

He looked down pointedly at my soaked sweater and dress. My nipples were poking at the dress, and I wrapped the cardigan over them. "You don't look fine," he said, raising his gaze to my soaked hair. "You look like you're having trouble getting a cab."

Through my anger, it took a second to catch on, but that was when I realized: *this* was the game.

I was a broke art student, trying to catch a taxi in the pouring rain. He was... whoever he was. I could stay mad, or I could get back into character and play.

It took only a second for me to think it through, a second that no onlooker would notice. But Aidan was so close, watching me so carefully, I knew he saw.

I bit my lip and watched his gaze fix on where my teeth bit my skin. "Okay, maybe I'm having a little trouble," I admitted. "I appreciate the umbrella. I'm getting really wet."

It was a classic double entendre, cheesy even. It worked. I could tell from the twitch in his jaw.

"Where are you headed?" he asked.

"Just to the subway," I replied. "I'm going home to the Bronx."

His eyebrows rose. "You're a Bronx girl?"

"Not really. I just live there with my roommate because the apartment was cheap."

He shook his head. "Well, you're not taking the subway there tonight. The subway is flooded with all this rain and half the lines are down."

That was probably a lie, though the New York Metro wasn't exactly known to be reliable. "Oh, shit," I said in distress, running a hand over my soaked hair. "How the hell am I supposed to get home? I can't afford a taxi the whole way."

"Let me help," he said. "My car and driver are pulling up any minute. I'll send him to take you home."

I gaped at him. "You can't do that. I mean, I can't ask you to. You don't even know me."

"My name is William." He held his hand out. The rain pounded the umbrella, loud and insistent. Water was splashing my legs, and probably his too.

I bit my lip again, because Rachel would think twice. Then I took his hand and shook it. "I'm Rachel," I said. "I'm an art student."

"And I work in boring old banking." He smiled and let me go, but before his hand left mine I felt it—that crazy *zing*, that wild pulse of attraction. I swallowed, and he watched.

"Were you, um, were you at the show?" I asked. My skin was getting hot under his gaze, and I wondered if he could tell in the dark.

He glanced behind us at the gallery. "Not really. That is, not as an art lover. I was here more in a landlord capacity."

I gaped at him again. "You *own* the gallery?"

"I own the building. It's one of my better investments." He looked at my surprised face, then shrugged. "Real estate is a sideline of mine. It seems I have a knack for it."

I wondered suddenly if Tower VC actually owned the gallery behind me. It was entirely possible. If so, then Aidan was playing it close to his real self tonight. "Do you like it?" I asked him. "Banking and real estate, I mean. Do you like it?"

"It makes money, but it's utterly cold and unfulfilling," he replied bluntly. "But it doesn't matter, really. I've never met anyone who actually likes what they do."

"I do." As both Rachel and Samantha, I meant it. "I like what I do."

He leaned closer. I could smell his scent mixed with rain, and the mixture made my blood pound. He reached up and touched his thumb to my cheek, brushing away a drop of water that had blown there. "Then you're fascinating, Rachel," he said, his voice low. "At least to me."

We stood there, our gazes locked, and I felt the same way I had the last time, when we'd played the game. I let myself feel the pure intoxication of being close to him, of wanting him. Of knowing that he wanted me. My body throbbed, and I felt purely alive. This gorgeous man was going to have me. I wasn't sure where or how, which made it thrilling. I just knew it was going to happen, and it was going to be amazing.

I never wanted this game to end.

"Here's my car," William said, breaking the moment. A car pulled up at the curb, and he opened the back door and helped me in, folding the umbrella as he got in himself. "We'll go uptown first, so I can get out at my place. Then I'll have him take you wherever you need to go. If that's okay with you, of course."

I fidgeted as he closed the door. He was big and close in the car, his body brushing mine. "You really don't have to do this," I said again.

"Anything to help a lady in distress," he said.

The car pulled into traffic, the rain pounding on the roof and the windows. Lightning flashed and thunder rolled high above, the storm showing no signs of letting up.

My clothes were cold and wet against my skin, and I shivered. My nipples were hard beneath my dress and my thighs had goosebumps. Without thinking, I inched closer to the man next to me, seeking his body warmth. I felt his muscles tense briefly in surprise, then relax again. He didn't resist.

We rode in silence for a minute, and then he said, "If you don't have cab fare, how did you afford the ticket to the exhibit?"

"It was my roommate's," I said. "She got it because she knows one of the artists. But she has the flu, so she gave it to me."

"You're very lucky, then," he said softly.

"Yes, I'm very lucky."

I burrowed a little closer to him, and he put a hand over mine, touching the backs of my fingers. I felt it like an electric pulse everywhere. "Your hands are cold," he said.

"I'll be okay."

"All of you is cold."

"A little."

I wondered how it would happen. Where would he take me? Did I need to be more forward? I'd been forward the last time, bold. I watched him closely for cues about how he wanted me to be.

He kept his hand on mine, his warm fingers against my skin. "Listen," he said. "You're soaked and freezing. Why don't you come and dry off in my apartment for a little while before I send you home?"

And there it was. My cue.

"Yes," I said. "I'd love to."

TWENTY-FIVE

Aidan

SHE WAS PERFECT. She was always perfect, whether she was Rachel or Samantha or anyone else. Tonight she'd left off the bold eye makeup and was a beautiful waif, a pretty art student stranded in the rain. And she was going to be mine.

I left my hand on hers for the rest of the ride, and we didn't speak. When we got to the Upper East Side she put my hand on her knee, just under the hem of her dress, and left it there. I could feel the warm pulse of her skin against mine.

I brought her to my penthouse—it was part of the reason I'd sent her here earlier this week. I'd wanted her to know this was where I lived, that when we did this I was bringing her to my home. She'd also know not to let on. So did I.

I led her out of the car. My driver, Edward, had basic instructions. He didn't ask questions, which I approved of. Since I never had women at my apartment, this wasn't a familiar routine, but he was a professional and he played along in silence. I paid him well, and I silently promised him a bonus.

Rachel crossed her arms over her chest while we were in the elevator, hugging herself. She looked damp and messy and completely exquisite. She also looked every bit the art student, and not like the polished professional I saw every day. As for me, tonight I was playing someone almost uncomfortably close to myself. I didn't want to examine too closely why that was. I could have pretended to be anyone, yet I'd chosen a man who dealt in real estate and lived in my apartment. If I was going to nitpick that, I'd think that maybe I wanted this woman for myself, the game be damned. So I didn't nitpick it.

Rachel walked into my apartment and looked around, wide-eyed, looking convincingly like she'd never seen the place before. "This is amazing," she said.

"Feel free to tidy up," I said. "There are clean towels in the bathroom. I'll get us a drink."

She disappeared into the bathroom, and I heard the tap running. I knew I'd surprised her when I showed up with that umbrella, and I congratulated myself for it. She had no idea I'd been at the art show, watching out of her line of sight. I didn't want to be seen talking to her and leaving with her when there was a chance someone could recognize me. When she looked like she was about to leave, I'd made my play. It was a gamble that might not have worked, but I'd been lucky.

I took off my wet shoes and socks in the bedroom and changed into worn jeans and an old NYU T-shirt. I'd never been to NYU, but William had. He was a smart man who had earned his way in the world, not a former fucked-up teenager who had lucked into millions of dollars and a career. When I played a role, I always left that fucked-up teenager behind.

Rachel was still in the bathroom, so I walked barefoot into the kitchen and poured two glasses of wine. I carried them to the main room and sat on the sofa, waiting.

She took her time, and when she came out, I saw why. She was dried off now, her hair down. She was also naked, wearing nothing but one of my large, white towels wrapped around herself.

She stepped into the main room, her cheeks flushing. "I hope you don't mind," she said. "There's a heated towel rack in the bathroom. I put my clothes on it."

I looked at her lean legs, her perfect shoulders. "I don't mind." I put my glass down and leaned forward. "Come here."

She shifted, but she was watching me, her gaze hungry. "I realize we don't know each other, but—"

"Come here."

She stepped forward. It was a scene out of a fantasy, watching her come closer. Something that would never happen with an actual stranger in real life. For me, it could only happen with Samantha.

But no, she wasn't Samantha. I needed to think of her as Rachel. I had to remind myself of that.

I held out my hand, and she took it. I tugged her gently, and she came. Thunder rolled out the window, moving away now. With a sigh, she straddled my lap and lowered herself onto it.

She was warm, damp, perfect woman. I remembered the dip of her clavicle from last time, the intoxicating smell of her skin. She was bare under the towel, her pussy bare against my jeans. She settled further, gripping my hips with her knees.

I reached my hand to the back of her head, pulled her down gently, and kissed her.

I remembered this, too. Samantha—Rachel—had a soft mouth and a flavor so intense it made me ache. She opened her mouth and I licked inside, tasting her, exploring her. She squirmed against me, impatient and needy. I'd kept her in suspense. I'd made her wait, and she was more than ready.

I slid my hand under the towel, finding her wet and slick. I stroked her once with my fingertips as she moaned in my mouth. "Is this what you want?" I asked her, breaking the kiss.

"Yes," she sighed.

"Say it."

"I want that. I want it."

"Drop the towel."

She did, and now she was naked, every delicious and perfect curve of her on my lap, like a dessert I didn't remotely deserve. I stroked my hands over her hips and she tugged my shirt up, moving fast and almost clumsy. I pulled it off over my head and dropped it. Then I pulled her in for another kiss.

She nipped my lip, impatient. I stroked her breasts—I remembered those from last time, too—and her hands dug down to the buttons of my jeans, undoing them, her fingers working their way inside. *The longer you make this woman wait,* I told myself, *the hotter she burns.* I wouldn't forget it.

I lifted my hips and she shoved my jeans down, just enough to free my cock. She readjusted herself on my thighs and stroked it. I broke the kiss and ran my thumb over her reddened bottom lip, using every drop of my strength to maintain control. "Is that what you want?" I asked her.

"Yes," she breathed.

"Say it."

She stroked me. "This. I want this."

"How much do you want it?"

Her eyes fluttered shut, maybe in embarrassment, maybe in desire. Maybe both. "I want it very, very much."

I took a condom from my jeans pocket and opened it. I put my hand over hers and we both put it on me. Then I leaned forward and sucked on the skin of her neck, tasting her damp flavor, using just enough pressure to make it almost hurt. "Take what you want," I told her.

She put her hands on my bare shoulders and rose up on her knees, then lowered herself down on me. We both made some kind of sound, half pleasure and half pain. A week. It had been a week since I'd been inside this woman, and I hadn't let myself feel the lack of it. I hadn't let myself remember how hot she was, how tight, how everything went away when I was sunk inside her. I hadn't been allowed to feel that, so I hadn't. Not until I was inside her again.

She moved on me, and I gripped her hips. *The condom has to go,* I thought, the idea coming from nowhere. I'd never had bare sex, but I absolutely had to have it with this woman. I filed that away as a problem I'd find a solution to.

"Oh, God," she said, and I knew she was feeling the same way I was, the satisfaction of a deep, impossible craving. I leaned up and sucked on her neck again, making her flinch. I didn't want to leave a visible mark, but I pushed it as close as I could. In response she moved on my lap, making me sink deeper. We both moaned.

"Incredible," I said against her skin. "You are so fucking incredible."

She moved her hips, her eyes drifting shut as my fingers dug into her hips. Her body moved in a rhythm, sliding on me, her knees sinking into the sofa.

"That's it," I coaxed her softly. "Please yourself." It pleased me to watch it, to feel it. I slid my hand down her belly, finding her clit with my thumb. I rubbed it with just the right pressure, on just the right spot, as she moved over and over.

I felt the orgasm inside her first, a shaking tremor, and then she was crying out and gripping my shoulders, unable to stop herself. My own orgasm hit like a freight train and I emptied myself into her. Then we both collapsed, panting and sweating.

In that moment, I wanted to keep her. I wanted to have her. I wanted her to be mine—not the just the pretend woman, but the real one. I would have done anything.

She lifted her head and looked into my eyes. She looked dazed, pleased, and completely satisfied. She smiled at me, and the smile was so beautiful I felt it in my bones.

"Thank you," she said. "I guess it's time for me to leave."

TWENTY-SIX

Samantha

"I'M TELLING YOU, there's something going on with him," Jade, the receptionist at Tower VC, said as she poured her coffee. "But no one knows what it is."

"I don't know." This was Anita, the intern in the legal department. She was sipping her coffee, frowning as she scrolled on her phone. "I don't see what you're talking about."

"Keep scrolling," Jade said.

I took a cup and poured my coffee. There was no one else at the coffee station in the office, and no one within earshot. Still, I leaned a little closer. "What don't you see?" I asked.

Jade raised an eyebrow at me. She was twenty-two, black, tall, and gorgeous. "Busted," she said. "If we show you, you have to promise not to tell the boss."

"Of course I won't tell him," I said, suppressing the flutter in my chest, and the second one lower down. Aidan wasn't in the office today—he had back-to-back real estate meetings around town. It was Tuesday, and I hadn't seen him since Saturday night. The night that hadn't happened, of course. At least, not to me.

I couldn't think about it right now. These were my coworkers, and Jade was watching me. "I pinky swear," I said to her.

"You know Aidan doesn't like gossip," Jade said.

I felt my stomach twist. Gossip?

"I don't see any gossip," Anita said. "Maybe they took it down."

"It's there." Jade leaned over to Anita's phone, scrolled quickly. "See? There. Read it."

"'What a surprise to see a face we knew at the Masoku Gallery on Saturday night,'" Anita read aloud. "'The Man in Black himself, Aidan Winters, made an appearance. But he wasn't wearing his signature black! He swapped his usual severe clothes for gray. Why? Your guess is as good as ours! Though we shouldn't be too surprised to see Mr. Winters on the premises, since his multimillion-dollar company, Tower VC, owns the building and invested in the gallery. He never appears at the gallery's shows, so we didn't know he was an art lover. Did a woman lure him there? We'd love to know. There were no photos allowed, so you'll have to take our word for it. In the meantime, the Man in Black maintains his bachelor status—and his air of mystery!'"

"Stupid, I know," Jade said. "Still, he's been different lately. I've definitely noticed."

"It was just an art show," Anita said.

"He didn't wear black," Jade said. "Have you ever seen him wear anything but black?"

"No, but I like it. He always looks hot."

They looked at me, expecting me to say something. Anything.

And for a second, I couldn't think. My brain went blank and my hands went cold.

Aidan had been seen at the art show. There was gossip about it. That was why he hadn't approached me inside the gallery—because he'd known there was a risk.

A risk I had taken without thinking.

And Tower VC really did own the building. That hadn't been part of the game.

The silence had gone on a little too long, and both women were looking at me, so I said, "I've never seen him wear anything but black, either."

Because I was Samantha, and for Samantha, that was true.

"Come on," Jade said. "You work with him more than the rest of us. You have to have noticed his mood."

"His mood?" I asked.

"He was completely impossible after the Chicago trip," Anita said, nodding. "I remember that. But then he mellowed out."

"Mellow for Aidan, that is," Jade agreed. "He's still his scary-ass self, but something's different. I know the look of a man who's getting some, and trust me, that man is definitely getting some. I'd bet a million bucks."

I put my coffee to my lips and sipped it. Hard.

"Damn, that is one lucky woman," Anita said. She gestured to the article on her phone. "An artist, right? That's why he showed up at the show all casual. He's got some artist chick and he's banging her senseless."

"Maybe." Jade looked at me, an all-knowing look that demanded answers. "Spill it, Samantha. You know the dirt."

I put my coffee down. I had to get control, and I had to do it now. "I don't know anything," I said, shrugging. "You know he doesn't tell me his personal life. He definitely wouldn't tell me that kind of detail."

"No, but you have eyes," Jade said. "Am I right or am I crazy?"

Why had I walked into this conversation? Oh right, because I was insatiably curious about anything to do with my boss. Which now I was regretting. "I suppose he's in a good mood," I said, "though he's always very professional with me."

There. That was a good answer. The answer a proper executive assistant would give.

"You mark my words," Jade said. "There's something going on. And sooner or later the gossip sites are going to pick it up. Then you'll see some fireworks."

I WAS IN MY OFFICE, scanning contracts for the confidential server, when my phone rang. It was Aidan.

"What's up?" I asked him when I answered.

"Come outside," he said. "I want you to come with me."

"Go with you where?"

"I want your opinion on something."

"All right. Give me a minute." I hung up, locked my office, and took the elevator to the ground floor. It was a beautiful day—the rain had cleared the skies, and a warm breeze was blowing. June was finally here. In a month, New York would be hot and unbearable, mostly smelling like rank sweat and garbage, but today it was a nice place to be.

Aidan's company car and driver had pulled up to the curb. He pushed open the back door and gestured me to get in.

"This is a little mafia-like," I said as I got in.

"Hardly," Aidan said. He was wearing his signature black, his laptop open on his lap. Aidan tended to work in the car while on the way to meetings—he said it was the best way not to waste time. "It's just a meeting."

"With who?"

"An agent for the building we're thinking of buying. I can't decide if it's a good investment or not."

When he didn't continue, I filled in the blanks, incredulous. "You mean you want my opinion?"

"Yes, I do." Gone was the man who had picked me up on Saturday night. This was all-business Aidan, calm and impenetrable. His scary-ass self, as Jade said. He handed me some papers, and his knee brushed mine. I ignored the fact that my skin tingled with even that slight touch.

"These are building records," I said. I'd seen plenty of these since working for Aidan. "We're going to the Lower East Side?"

"One of Manhattan's resurging neighborhoods," Aidan said. "For decades one of the poorest parts of the city. Now being gentrified like everywhere else."

He didn't sound impressed. "You're not a fan?" I asked.

"Of the Lower East Side? Sure, especially the restaurants. Of gentrification? I'm not convinced every neighborhood needs a Sephora megastore and an artisanal juice bar. But who am I to dictate the free market?"

I liked Aidan when he was like this. It was always interesting to pick his brain. He wasn't college educated, which meant he sometimes knew unusual things. There was a moment of quiet in the car, and I found myself enjoying it—Aidan's presence next to me, his scent, his knee brushing mine. Saturday night had been incredible, but I also liked just being near him.

"I didn't know Tower VC owned the Masoku Gallery," I said.

His dark eyes flickered to me, and I saw something in their depths—he knew what I was getting at. "It's one of my favorite properties of ours, I admit," he said. "It doesn't generate the most profit, but it's a place that makes the neighborhood unique and interesting."

I looked casually down at my papers. "You were spotted there by the gossip sites on Saturday night. They said you weren't wearing black."

He was quiet for a second. "I wasn't. I told you I own other colors."

"Still, since we're in private here I thought I should warn you. If you don't want to be seen, you need to be more careful."

"Noted," he said.

I raised my gaze to him again. He was looking at me.

"It was something of an impulse," he said gently. "I like the people who come to the gallery."

I bit my lip. "There's gossip at the office, too, as long as I'm warning you. People think you're seeing someone."

He looked a little icy at that. "If I am, it's nobody's business."

"True. But the rumor is that you're..." I trailed off.

Aidan raised his eyebrows. "That I'm what?"

I cleared my throat. "That you're getting laid."

He scratched his chin for a second, thinking that over. "Offices are the worst fucking places, I swear to God," he said. "Is anyone talking about you?"

It was the closest he'd come to alluding to what we did in our off-hours. "No one is talking about me that I can tell," I said. "Certainly not to my face."

"All right, then. But you're right. I'll be more discreet. In the meantime, tell me whether, if you had twenty million dollars, you'd buy this building or not."

"I DON'T KNOW," I said when we had finished the tour of the building. "I'm not an expert."

The real estate agent had left, and we were standing in front of the building, looking up at it. It was in rough shape, there was no doubt—the building had been neglected for nearly ten years, and there was water damage and bad electrical wiring. But it was in a good spot on the Lower East Side.

"I'm not an expert, either," Aidan said. "Do you want to know a secret? Most of the time I fucking guess."

"Then why don't you fucking guess this time?" I asked him.

He smiled at my profanity. He was flat-out gorgeous when he smiled, probably because it was so rare. "I don't know. I've been second-guessing myself lately—I'm not sure why. Maybe I'm burned out."

He was serious, so I gave it a try. "Well, it's an eyesore," I said, looking at how the building compared to the others on the street. "I'm not sure the building should be saved, even if it could be. You might have to tear down and rebuild."

"So the property is twenty million, and rebuilding is another ten," Aidan said. "The question is, will it be worth at least thirty million when it's all over? Preferably forty, if I'm going to spend that kind of time."

I looked at it again. It was a four-story apartment building, empty now. I couldn't believe we were talking about twenty, thirty, forty million dollars as if it was pocket change. "You won't have any renters while you rebuild."

"Correct. No cash flow at all. Money going out and not coming in."

"Is it being sold for below market value?"

"This is Manhattan, so absolutely fucking not."

"But when it's finished and you get renters, then you make money."

"Over time, yes. Or I sell it and move on."

I looked up and down the street again. "This is a nice street," I said. "These are working people. There are bodegas and little restaurants. This building should be part of that, part of the neighborhood. Maybe row townhouses with young families in them. It would add to the community."

I stopped talking, because he was looking at me. I couldn't decipher his expression. "What?" I said.

"You're sentimental," Aidan replied. "You're a romantic."

"I'm not," I protested. "You're the one who said the art gallery added to the neighborhood."

"I bought the art gallery for a song, and it's gone significantly up in value."

"Value you only realize if you sell it."

"And I'm not selling," Aidan agreed. "But I could."

I crossed my arms. "I'm not an expert, like I said. But it seems to me that real estate is about more than just making money. It's about making a neighborhood where people want to live, to work. Where businesses can open and make a profit. Where, I don't know, where people could live good lives."

"And my goal is to make money," Aidan said. "As much money as humanly possible, and then even more."

I thought of the Aidan I'd met on Saturday night, who had called himself William. *It's utterly cold and unfulfilling*, he'd said of real estate. "I don't believe you just want to make money," I said.

"Oh no?" His voice was icy again. "Then what do I want?"

"I don't know. Something else. Something that has meaning."

He didn't answer that. "And what do you want?" he asked me.

I shook my head. "Nothing. I told you my story. Since I was a baby, I've been lucky to be alive. Things have turned out better for me than they had any right to."

"So you don't want anything at all?"

"I want safety and security," I said. "I want a job that fulfills me and pays the bills. I want my sister nearby and reasonably happy. I have those things. What else could I want?"

The words hung there. After a moment, Aidan nodded.

"All right," he said. "We'll see."

THE TEXT CAME AT MIDNIGHT. I was alone in my condo, sitting in bed, reading. The book was *One Night with the Devil*, and to be completely honest it was the third time I'd read it. Especially the scene where the hero stripped the heroine naked, tied a silk rope around her wrists, put her on all fours on the bed, and—

On the nightstand, my phone buzzed. I picked it up and read the text from Aidan.

Tomorrow night, Shaker's rooftop on Fifth Avenue. Just after nine.

My throat went dry. Underneath my sleep T-shirt, my nipples hardened. I put my book down.

Yes, I replied.

I didn't even think of saying no.

Because damn it, Aidan Winters was right. There was something else I wanted, after all.

TWENTY-SEVEN

Samantha

THE JACQUES WAS CLASSY, but Shaker's was trendy, expensive, and crowded. It was on the roof of an office building, twelve stories up. Fifth Avenue stretched away below, surrounded by skyscrapers—the view dominated by the Empire State Building, still Art Deco perfection after so many years.

It was a beautiful night when I arrived—just after nine, as instructed. The days were getting longer, and the sun had set just a little while ago. A warm breeze blew and the New Yorkers who were drinking up here, high above the city, were just warming up. I threaded my way through them and walked to the bar.

Aidan was there.

I had to pause for a minute, because he was sitting on a bar stool, drinking a glass of whiskey, wearing jeans and a T-shirt. *Jeans and a T-shirt.* The jeans were worn, and the shirt was light gray, fitting him to perfection. His biceps—had I ever noticed

Aidan's biceps before? I noticed them now. They were perfectly shaped and hard as granite. The shirt fell straight over his flat stomach. The line of his shoulders was to die for.

He was gorgeous in a suit, and he was gorgeous in jeans and a tee. It wasn't fair.

No one was looking at him, except for a couple of women who were checking him out. He was hot, but he wasn't recognized as the Man in Black. I took a breath and got into character, preparing to play the game once again.

I was wearing a skirt, blouse, and heels. My name was Leigh, and I'd just left the office after working late. I had recently been dumped by my long-term boyfriend, who I'd thought would marry me, and I was low on confidence but determined to get back into the dating pool and meet someone. Tonight I screwed up my courage to approach the hot guy in jeans sitting alone at the bar.

A seat opened up next to him and I grabbed it. I signaled the bartender and ordered a glass of white wine spritzer.

As the bartender pushed the drink my way, Aidan turned and looked at me. He smiled appreciatively—a cocky grin. God, he was so gorgeous.

"Hi there, Spritzer Girl," he said.

"Hi, Whiskey Guy," I replied.

And just like that, the game was on.

His name was Max, and he was an airline pilot on leave. In fact, he had to be at JFK in a few hours for a trip to Seoul. He was hot and very, very aware of it. He was looking for a gorgeous woman to spend time with before he left again, and he said I fit the bill.

I told him my story—the breakup, the late-night working. "I don't usually work so late," I said, "but my boss wouldn't let me leave."

"Your boss sounds demanding," Max said.

I looked at his familiar dark eyes, feeling myself smile. "He's not an asshole, not really. He's just moody."

His eyebrows went up. He was definitely interested in this topic. "You think he's moody?"

"Sure he is. He's rich, but he hasn't always been rich. He isn't spoiled—part of him is still rough. When he's in a good mood, he's nice. But then he gets dark. For example, there was an entire week when he barely spoke to me."

Max frowned, ready to argue. "He probably had a good reason."

"No, he didn't." I was enjoying this. I took another sip of my spritzer. "Everyone in the office is terrified of him. No one wants to cross him. I've never seen it happen, but I know it's bad."

"Um." Max cleared his throat. "Well, maybe the guy is under a lot of stress."

"Maybe. It doesn't make him any less intimidating, though."

He looked at me in shock. "Your boss intimidates you?"

I laughed. "Of course he does. He's intimidated me since the first minute I met him. I can't believe I've worked for him all this time and he hasn't caught on."

There was a second of silence between us, louder than any of the laughter at the bar. Just him and me and the air practically shimmering. I could feel every part of my body, my blood pulsing, the breeze on my skin.

"You know what, Leigh?" he said at last.

I shivered. "What?"

"I feel bad for you, working for this guy. Dealing with his moods and his intimidation. Staying at the office until nine at night. I think you need to release some tension."

I could feel his gaze on me like a touch, brushing along my neck, down past my collarbones. "I could do that," I said slowly. "Release tension."

"Good, because I have an idea."

That was how we ended up in one of the bathrooms ten minutes later. The bathrooms at Shaker's, it turned out, were beautifully decorated and incredibly clean. And private. Especially the one at the very back of the last corridor, where it seemed that no one else went.

Max—Aidan—pressed me against the counter, his strong arms boxing me in, his hips against mine, his lips moving expertly up my neck. Familiar and unfamiliar at the same time. I could feel his rough jeans through my skirt. I had never done anything like this before, but I let my head fall back, let my eyes close. "How much time do we have?" I breathed.

"Fifteen minutes, maybe," was the answer against my skin. "Twenty tops."

"I don't think—"

"Don't think. Relax. I'll take care of it. Tension release, remember?"

His mouth took mine, tasting of warm man and whiskey. His teeth raked against my lip and I felt the sting through my body, down between my legs. His hands moved to my skirt, pulling it up gently and then pulling my panties down.

I felt my fingers dig into the hard muscles of his shoulders. *Aidan,* I thought crazily. *This is Aidan, the man I went to look at real estate with the other day. The man I see at the office almost every day.* The man who had given me the orgasm of my life just by sitting on his sofa with me naked in his lap. That had been so intense I'd been dazed. I barely remembered leaving, had no idea what I'd said. I had the feeling I'd done it wrong somehow, but it hadn't occurred to me until I was sitting in Aidan's hired car, his driver taking me home in the rain.

If I'd done something wrong that night, he'd obviously forgiven me.

This wasn't me, this office girl who let herself get seduced by a cocky pilot, who was locked in a public bathroom with her panties on the floor and a man's gorgeous hands lifting her skirt up. Except for in my fantasies, this had never, ever been me.

The still-functioning fragments of my brain managed to remember something practical. "Do you have a condom?" I asked.

"Don't need one," he said against my mouth.

"But—"

"I've got it handled. Relax."

I was going to argue, but then I saw what he meant. Because he put his hands on my hips, lifting me to the counter. Then he lowered to his knees.

I had definitely, *definitely* never done this.

Hardly ever, in regular circumstances. And never in public, fully dressed except for my panties, with a stranger.

But his touch was familiar as he pushed my knees apart. And even though he'd never done this to me before, his mouth still felt familiar when he licked between my legs.

I gasped aloud, my hands gripping the edge of the counter, my hips lifting off. Flinching and at the same time wanting more. The reaction I always had when he touched me there.

He took it as an invitation.

He was right.

How did he know what to do? Because he knew exactly what pressure to put where, exactly how hard, for exactly how long. He knew how to make me crazy, how to make me lose my dignity. Ten minutes ago, I'd never done this and as far as I knew, I never would. Now I had my legs open in a bathroom and I was going to come, fast and hard, dirty and intense, and it was pure bliss.

He was as good as his word. I bit my lips, trying not to cry out as the orgasm hit me, shaking me to my core. He was merciless all the way through, teasing every ripple out of me. Then, instead of taking pity on me, he slipped his fingers through my hot flesh and rubbed me, punctuating the movement with his tongue. I moaned in surrender, and incredibly, I felt the pressure building again. I gave in to it, letting him do everything he wanted, feeling the pleasure go up and up, tighter and tighter, until I came a second time.

When I was finally finished and coming down, he backed away and put the hem of my skirt down, almost polite.

He stood, picking up my panties from the floor. He was unbearably beautiful in that moment, sexy and dirty and daring. I couldn't take my eyes off him. My entire body was high with bliss. I had never seen a more perfect man in my life.

He's mine, I thought. *He has to be.*

He put my panties in my hand. "Stress relief, like I promised," he said. For a second I thought he was going to lean in and kiss me, but instead he smiled. I could have sworn that something behind that smile was a little sad.

"Thank you. Time for me to leave," he said.

By the time I remembered that was what I'd said to him the last time, the door had already closed behind him.

TWENTY-EIGHT

Aidan

IT WAS six thirty in the morning. I was at the gym in my building and I had just finished my workout—I was covered in sweat—when my phone rang. It was Alex. I mopped my forehead with a towel and answered it.

"It's done," Alex said. "I found our missing computer programmer and got him out of his hidey hole. I got him to talk about the Egerton brothers and their app."

"And?"

"And yes, they definitely stole the code. He had a lawsuit set to go against them and everything. He was going to win. But the Egertons convinced him to drop it."

"How the hell did they do that?"

"Money, and lots of it. They also threatened to tell his current girlfriend about his previous girlfriend's abortion. These programmers all know each other, and they know each other's dirty secrets."

"What a couple of assholes," I said. "I don't regret taking them down now."

"You didn't regret it before, Aidan."

"True." I thought it over. "So he took the money under the table, but he didn't sign anything."

"No NDA, no nothing. Not a damn thing. Which makes them a couple of very stupid assholes."

I stood and left the gym, heading for the elevator. "You convinced him to talk?"

"It wasn't hard. He knows they're going to take the company public and make hundreds of millions. It's been a few years since he took the deal, and he's bitter about it. He has a lot to say."

"And the girlfriend?" I asked as the elevator doors closed.

"She's his wife now, and they have a kid. The ex-girlfriend is a nonissue by this point. Oh, and he's sick of Florida. He hates it there. Having just spent a week there, I don't blame him."

"Get him to New York, all expenses paid," I said. "His wife and child, too. I'll get our lawyers to depose him. I'll call some of my contacts at the Federal Trade Commission. I think they'll be interested to know what the Egertons are hiding from potential investors before they go public."

"You know, at first I thought you were crazy," Alex said. "Going after these guys because of a couple of comments? I know they were out of line, but it seemed like you were overreacting. But now that I've learned what scumbags the Egertons are, I'm all for it. Let's see if we can burn them down."

I walked into my penthouse to shower and get dressed for work. "I just look nice. You know that."

"True. You might wear a suit, but you can't take the Chicago kid out of you, Aidan. Deep down, you're still that kid I met when we were fifteen, who was ready to fight anyone who pissed him off."

I pulled my sweaty shirt off over my head and dumped it in the hamper, then put the phone back to my ear. "Speaking of which, I have an idea about Noah's Chicago project."

"Yeah, that," Alex said. He'd voted against it, just like I had. "Are you changing your mind? You want to invest in a rundown old building for sentimental reasons?"

"I've been looking over some of the data," I said. "Noah might be right. It has potential other than the fact that we lived there."

"I know that neighborhood, Aidan. That building is a charity project. And we're not in the business of charity."

I thought of standing on a street on the Lower East Side with Samantha, looking at a building through her eyes and seeing something I wasn't used to seeing. "I think we can do more than just make money," I said to Alex. "And you won't have to do anything."

"All right, I'm listening."

So I told him my idea. He was quiet while I talked, and quiet when I finished. Quiet for too long.

"Well?" I said. "What do you think?"

"I've never heard you come up with anything like this," Alex said.

"That isn't an answer. Yes or no?"

"I don't hate it," he admitted. "At least, not completely. Do you think Noah and Dane will go for it?"

I wasn't sure at all, but I said, "Yes."

"Liar. Okay, fine. You have my vote. If you can convince the other two, then do it."

I grinned. "I knew you'd come around."

"There's one other person you have to convince," Alex said. "Good luck with it." He hung up.

AFTER OUR LAST ENCOUNTER, I wasn't sure what Samantha thought of me. I had no doubt that we'd played the game to perfection, and absolutely no doubt that I'd pleased her—I'd left her in an orgasmic puddle in the bathroom at Shaker's. And yes, I was pretty fucking proud of it.

But the way I left was abrupt. That was on purpose, to remind her that she wasn't in complete control of this game, that she didn't hold all the cards. That playing required both of us. She had left me at a disadvantage after the night at the art gallery —I'd been shaken by that encounter, pushed off-balance. I'd been dying for her, and she hadn't noticed. I didn't particularly like feeling like she had me at her back and call—and she didn't even know it. Turnabout was fair play.

By eight thirty I was dressed in my usual black—it was warm today, so I wore dress pants and a shirt but had left off my jacket —and I was in the lobby of the office, waiting for the elevator. I heard heels clicking softly on the marble behind me, and I smelled a familiar scent. In the space of a second, I knew who it was.

Samantha came to stand beside me, waiting. She was wearing a dark blue short-sleeved button-up dress, her hair up in its usual professional twist. Her makeup was subtle and lovely as always. And she wore low heels with ankle straps.

My gaze dropped to the shoes—those sexy shoes—and then the dress. My sexual fantasies had been right. She looked incredible in blue.

I raised my gaze to her profile. She was staring fixedly at the elevator button. There was a pink flush on her cheekbones that wasn't blush.

"Good morning, Samantha," I said.

She cleared her throat, soft and ladylike. "Good morning, Aidan."

Still she wouldn't look at me. I remembered pushing her skirt up, pushing her thighs apart, and tasting her. I remembered what she tasted like and the sounds she made. I remembered making her come. Twice.

I could tell she was remembering the same thing. She just wasn't going to admit it.

Right there, in that moment, was when I decided to push her to the edge. Over it, if possible. I wanted to see how far we could go.

I glanced behind me to check that no one was in earshot, that the security guard was sitting behind his desk, looking somewhere else. Then I dropped my voice and said, "Honey."

Samantha started, blinked. She looked at me. "What?"

"Honey," I said. "That's what you tasted like."

Her eyes widened. Her mouth actually opened as her jaw dropped. Then the elevator dinged, the doors opening.

I put a hand to Samantha's elbow and guided her in, then pressed the button. The doors closed and we were alone.

Now her neck was flushing red. "We're at work," she said. "You can't say things like that."

"Yes, I can. It's an astute observation, considering I could still taste you when I got home last night. I replayed the sounds you make when you come while I jerked off in the shower."

"Aidan." She swallowed her shock and pressed her lips together. "I suppose I'm glad you enjoyed it. You certainly left fast enough."

I glanced at her. We were standing shoulder to shoulder, almost touching but not quite. She wasn't looking at me. "You didn't like that?" I asked.

Her lips thinned even more. "Was I supposed to?"

"I don't know. You're the queen of fast exits."

The doors opened on our floor. Samantha strode out, across the open office. I followed her. The receptionist was at her desk and a few other people were working. If they watched us, I didn't notice.

She unlocked her office and ducked inside, but I stood in the doorway before she could shut me out. I leaned on the doorframe and watched her put down her purse. "Don't you have your own office to go to?" she asked.

"I'm the boss," I reminded her. "Look at me."

"Aidan, this is completely—"

"Look at me."

She finally turned and faced me, flustered, her skin flushed. She was beautiful. So fucking beautiful.

I wanted her. I wanted Samantha. Rules or no rules. She was what I wanted.

"I think we're going to renegotiate the game," I said.

Now she started to look outraged. "We're not renegotiating. And we can't do it here."

"Where, if not here? My place? I'm up for it. You already have the codes to my penthouse."

"Are you being a pig on purpose, or is it just your natural state?"

"I'm being your boss and the man who plays your game whenever you want it."

"*My* game?" she said. "It's your game, too."

She was right. I'd liked being a pilot, picking up an office girl while he was in town for a few hours. I'd liked being an art dealer and a stranger picking up a girl in the rain, too. But the game, for me, wasn't the end goal. I knew that now. Samantha was the end goal.

I hadn't always gotten what I wanted in life. In fact, I rarely had. Strange thing for a rich man to say, but true. If I wanted

Samantha, I already knew I'd have to work for it. And I already knew she'd be worth it.

But first, we had to discuss the game.

"Meet in my office," I told her. "You have ten minutes."

She was still staring at me as I walked out the door.

TWENTY-NINE

Samantha

I DIDN'T GO to his office in ten minutes. Or twenty. Or forty.

I made him wait an hour.

Was it petty? Yes, it was. Was it childish? Yes, it was. Was it just a way to see if I could push his buttons the way he'd pushed mine? Definitely.

But damn it, he'd broken the rules. We'd set the game up perfectly and we'd played it without a hitch—this strange thing that satisfied both of us. We were in sync. And then he'd told me that I tasted like honey—right here in the elevator at work.

And it had made my heart beat faster and my breath come short, just like the game did.

That wasn't how it was supposed to work.

I had spent all of last night thinking about how he'd left me at Shaker's, the words he'd used. The slightly sad look in his eyes when he said them. And I realized that somewhere along the way, I'd screwed up. I'd misread him. We weren't as in sync as I thought we were.

We'd made a strict rule never to talk about the rules of the game. That back-and-forth, chess-match aspect had made things more exciting. But it had also meant he couldn't tell me I'd been a jerk in the usual way. So he'd done it by getting me off twice in a restaurant bathroom, then leaving.

Okay, I had to address what had happened. But I didn't have to jump when Aidan snapped his fingers, boss or not. We'd never had that relationship before the game began. Just because he'd given me the best, most intense orgasms of my life didn't mean that we'd have that relationship now. I was still his executive assistant, the best one at Executive Ranks. I wasn't his minion. I would go to his office, but I would do it on my time.

So I poured a coffee at the coffee station in the middle of the office and I drank it as I sorted email, both mine and his. I fielded requests for Aidan to take meetings or speak at conferences. I took a call from the legal department. I went through the mail.

There was a piece of mail from a hospital in Chicago. Thinking it was a request for a donation, I opened the letter and skimmed it. Too late, I realized how personal it was—I couldn't unread what I had read. I set the letter aside, along with other papers that I needed Aidan to sign. I went to his office and knocked on the door.

"Come in," he said.

I stepped in and closed the door behind me. Aidan was standing at his floor-to-ceiling windows, looking out at the city. He wasn't wearing a jacket or tie today, just black pants and a black dress shirt that was cut perfectly to his torso and the flaw-less line of his waist. His hands rested casually in his pockets. He had a shadow of stubble on his jaw. I let my gaze take him in for a quick second while he wasn't looking at me—the sinuous line of his muscled shoulders, the way his pants fit over his ass. I thought of the pilot I'd met in the bar last night, of how knowingly his mouth had worked over my pussy, and my skin went hot.

He turned and looked at me, his features stern. But I knew him now, and I could read his expression—there was amusement in his eyes. "Nice of you to show up," he said.

I kept my chin up. "Sorry, the time you gave didn't work for me. I had things to do."

"I apologize for keeping you from your important work."

He leaned his weight a little on one hip, and I thought of what he had looked like in jeans last night. I tried to keep my cool. "I went through the mail," I said. "There's a letter from a hospital. I'm sorry—I shouldn't have read it. I didn't know it was personal."

I held out the letter, but Aidan stayed where he was, making no move to take it. "Is it about my mother?" he asked.

"I don't know. I didn't read all of it."

"Read all of it now." His voice was calm, though cooler than before. "I don't want to read it. What do they want?"

I turned the page back around and read it. "They say, um, that in her condition she sometimes tries to wander from the grounds. They recommend moving her to a different section of the hospital where they watch the patients more closely."

There was not a hint of reaction in his face. "And?"

I read to the bottom. "And, er, the change in care is more expensive."

"Of course it is. Tell them that the change is fine and I approve the expense."

I folded the letter. "I'm sorry your mother is ill."

Pain showed in his expression for a brief moment and I watched him fight it back. I wondered how often he fought down his pain. "She's losing her memory," he said. "It's happening faster than the doctors expected, and they don't know why."

"What about your father?" I asked.

He shook his head. "My mother left my father when Ava and I were little after he hit her one too many times."

My stomach twisted. "I'm sorry, Aidan. I shouldn't pry."

"It isn't prying. Not when you know the person." He stepped toward me and touched the line of my jaw with his fingertip. "And I'd say we know each other pretty well, wouldn't you?"

I suppressed the shiver his touch gave me. Did we know each other really? We'd talked plenty, but that was usually in character. I raised my gaze to his. His eyes were dark and beautiful. There was pain in their depths but there was also warmth, because he was looking at me.

Yes, I did know this man. Even when we gave each other different names, I still knew him. And he knew me, in ways that no one else did—not my sister, my parents, my coworkers, my former lovers. Aidan knew me in a way that made me know myself better.

It was terrifying.

I was no one, an anonymous child who had been left at a hospital with her sister. Because I'd had to build my identity from nothing, I thrived on being the good daughter, the good sister, the good assistant. What Aidan knew about me—the real me—fractured all of that.

"I'm not renegotiating the game," I said.

Aidan's finger was still on my jaw. He dropped his hand. "Yes, you are."

"No, I'm not."

"Turn around."

It didn't matter how defiant or opinionated I was; when he said that, I did it. I didn't even think. I turned around.

His hands came to my hips. I sucked in a breath at the touch. I tried to keep it quiet, but he heard it. His fingers pressed into the fabric of my knee-length skirt, pulling it up one inch, and then another.

"Do you have any idea," he said, his voice low and rough, "how much I want to bend you over my desk and fuck you?"

I closed my eyes as I felt the hem of my skirt drift upward. "No," I said.

"You sound so convincing, Samantha, but we both know I could do it if I wanted. Undo the top button of your dress."

I did it, my hands moving of their own accord. My skin was flushing hot.

"The next one," Aidan said.

I unbuttoned the next one. Cool air brushed the skin between my breasts. The entire office was on the other side of the door—phones ringing, keyboards clicking. My pussy throbbed.

He lifted my skirt higher, then brushed his warm fingers over the outside of my thighs, tracing lines on my skin. "I would fuck you until you came," he said calmly. "I would fuck you until I came inside you, and you'd work the rest of the day knowing my cum was inside you. If you let me, I'd fuck you until I was the only thing you thought about every morning. I'd fuck you until you craved me above anything else."

A soft moan escaped my throat, but I cut it off. "No," I rasped.

His fingers moved to the front of my thighs, then traced a line between them. So very, very close to my pussy in my damp panties. "You won't let me, so I'm not going to. But you want me to, Samantha. You want me to fuck you, and you want it very badly."

"I don't." Who was I fooling? I was standing in Aidan's office, my dress unbuttoned and my skirt up, my eyes closed, dying for his hands between my legs. But I said it again. "I don't."

He leaned forward, his breath against my neck. I could smell him, the heady scent of him mixed with the smell of my own sex. "We don't need the game, Samantha," he said. "You don't need it. You never have. You just need to let go."

Behind my closed eyelids, I pictured that—what letting go would look like. What it would feel like. With Aidan, it would feel amazing, like I was finally myself after a lifetime of trying to be someone. Of not knowing who that woman really was.

I stood frozen and helpless, temptation washing over me. And then Aidan removed his hand. My body ached as he lowered my skirt, the fabric brushing my oversensitized legs. He circled to the front of me and gently fastened my buttons.

I opened my eyes and looked up at him. We looked like two people standing in an office, but he had just undone me completely, and we both knew it.

His expression was serious, his eyes dark. "Your move, Samantha," he said. "I'll be waiting."

THIRTY

Samantha

"I DON'T KNOW how you do that shit," Emma said to me. "I think I want to kill someone."

I raised my eyebrows as we walked into the smoothie bar on 8th. Just a few blocks from the Port Authority—historic home of junkies and prostitutes for most of New York's history—and an "artisanal smoothie" cost $13. "Murderous is not how you're supposed to feel after a yoga class," I told my sister. "That really isn't the point."

She rolled her eyes. Even in yoga pants and an expensive, complicated yoga top, Emma looked like she was on her way somewhere at top speed. "How does anyone do any of those poses? And why? I mean, triangle pose? I do *not* look like a triangle, no matter how you twist me. It isn't happening."

I grabbed her mint-and-kale smoothie and shoved it at her so she would stop complaining. I'd asked my sister out for a comfortable, relaxing Saturday, hoping for some girl time. But even though I loved my sister, girl time wasn't really her thing—evidenced by the fact that she had already pulled out her phone and was answering texts. Yoga wasn't Emma's thing, either, even though she was fit and strong.

"What?" she said, glancing up and noticing me looking at her.

I shrugged, sipping my own lemon-and-hand-pressed-cranberry smoothie. "I'm just wondering if you stay fit by crushing the bones of your enemies."

Emma grinned. "I also stay hydrated with their tears. It's part of my regime. Oh, and I run."

"Outside?"

She looked horrified. "Are you kidding? This is New York. I'd probably catch a communicable disease right before I got murdered. I do *not* have time for that."

There was a reason Emma was single and happy about it—most men found her a little terrifying. "How did it go with Ethan?" I asked her as we left the smoothie bar.

"Who?"

"The guy you tried to set me up with from Tinder. With the tattoos."

"Oh, him." She shrugged, though I thought her expression got a little tense. "It was fine, I guess. Nothing spectacular."

"So you slept with him, then."

"For the millionth time, Samantha, the word is *fucked.* And yes, I did."

My sister thought I was a square. She had no idea I'd come within seconds of fucking—yes, fucking—my smoking-hot boss in his office. I wasn't going to tell her. "And it was bad?" I asked.

"It was fine." Her voice was flat. "No fireworks, though, if you know what I mean."

I did. "For you or for him?"

Emma snorted. "Oh, there's always fireworks for the guy.

Every time. But for me, well, let's just say I'm glad I invested in a proper sex toy collection. Otherwise I'd be orgasmless and even more bitchy than I already am."

"You're not bitchy," I said loyally. "You're just driven. Focused."

"Thanks, sis." Emma smiled at me, one of her real smiles. It didn't matter that we were different—ever since we'd been left at that hospital, we'd been in this life together. We always would be. Even when she brushed me off.

Which she was about to do in three, two.... There it was. "I gotta go," she said, holding up her phone, as if that explained it. "Shit is hitting the fan. I'm going to go to the office and get some work done."

It was eleven o'clock on Saturday morning, but I already knew it was futile to tell my sister not to go to work. She'd ignore me anyway. "I thought we were going to go shopping," I said.

"I shop online. It's faster." Her phone buzzed again and she waved at me. "Later, sis."

I went back to my apartment, showered, and changed. Drank some water. Just a normal Saturday for a single working girl.

Your move, Samantha. I'll be waiting.

I put the glass of water down on the counter and took a breath. It was like Aidan was standing right there, saying it in my ear. My body flushed hot.

This had been happening ever since the scene in his office. I would be going about my life as normal, and then suddenly I'd be hot and aching, thinking about those words. I'd wake up thinking about them, my sheets twisted over my legs. I fell asleep thinking about them, too.

Aidan was as good as his word. He hadn't contacted me about anything other than the most mundane work issues. We hadn't been alone together. He hadn't texted me instructions for the next round of the game. Because, as he'd promised, the next round of the game was up to me.

You don't need the game. You never have. You just need to let go.

I was a coward. I knew that. I was pretending life was normal, that I hadn't played a wild and filthy game with my boss. I was pretending that it hadn't changed me, that it wasn't still changing me. My life wasn't normal while I was thinking about Aidan saying those words. It would never be normal until I had the guts to take the next step.

I sat down at my kitchen counter and my gaze caught on the erotic novel I'd bought. *One Night with the Devil.* The woman's hands on the cover, bound in red ribbon. I'd read the book multiple times by now—I could recite some of the passages by heart. It wasn't that I had a kink for being tied up and bound, though I knew some people did. What kept me coming back to the book was the boldness and fearlessness of it, of the heroine who craved pleasure and went after it with an incredibly hot man. *I don't care if it's one night or forever,* she tells him at one point. *I don't care if you keep me or you throw me away. I just want you to take me. Right now, in every way you desire. Take me.*

I had done that, been that way, with Aidan. During the game. I wasn't finished playing yet.

You don't need the game. You just need to let go.

I picked up my phone, and before I could lose my courage, I texted Aidan: *Where are you right now?*

His reply was typical Aidan, mysterious and sexy. *Does it matter? Now I'm talking to you.*

I swallowed, my throat dry. I should probably call him and talk about this in person, but my guts only took me so far. Besides, I didn't want to punctuate this with *um* and *uh* like a nervous idiot. I thought about Nadia, the heroine of *One Night with the Devil.* I thought of Sarah, the financial CEO I'd been in the first round of our game. She'd been sexy and proud of it, and I'd liked being her. I decided to channel her now.

I texted: *Are you still waiting for my signal?*

His reply was immediate: *Always.*

I smiled to myself. *I'll think about it,* I wrote, *but if we're going to renegotiate the game, I have conditions.*

The dots moved. *Name them.*

He was playing. I knew that—this was a different version of the game. But there was something raw and honest about it, too. I knew that right now, while not playing a role, Aidan would do anything I wanted.

I leaned back in my chair and sipped my water. *One of my favorite things about working for Tower VC,* I wrote, *is the health plan.*

Aidan: *Is that so?*

Me: *Yes. The prescription coverage is particularly generous. It's excellent for staying on birth control.*

There was a second of silence, and then the dots moved again. *Samantha, you are playing with fire.*

Of course, I wrote, *for me to consider any man, he'd have to have a clean bill of health. And I would provide the same.*

Aidan: *Hold that thought.*

I waited one minute, then two. I sipped my water. I was starting to get restless when my phone chimed again, this time with an email. I opened it and read it in shock.

Aidan had sent me exactly what I asked for—his clean bill of health, sent from his doctor. I scanned over the document and saw it was dated the day after we'd met at the art gallery. The last time we'd had sex with a condom.

He'd gone to the doctor the next day, because he'd planned this.

I opened my text app again.

Me: *Do you always get what you want?*

Aidan: *Your turn.*

Me: *You didn't answer my question.*

Aidan: *I'm not getting what I want right now, and I haven't in too long. You know that. Now send me the damned document.*

Me: *How do you know I have one?*

Aidan: *You wouldn't have started this conversation if you didn't. I'm waiting.*

Damn it, he was right. I'd had a checkup a month ago and had all of my annual tests done. I found the document he wanted and sent it in a reply email, then texted him again. *All right, now we're even.*

Aidan: *Done. Tell me your next condition.*

I bit my lip, my confidence ebbing. What was I doing? This man was my boss, one of the richest men in New York, and the sexiest man I'd ever met. I'd only been bold enough to seduce him when I was playing someone else.

I looked down at myself, sitting at my kitchen counter. I was wearing black leggings and a soft T-shirt with my most comfortable bra under it. My hair was in a rough ponytail and I had no makeup on. I didn't have on the heavy makeup and expensive dress I'd worn the first night of our game. I didn't have an identity at the ready. I was just me, on a Saturday morning. Did I actually think I could get a man like Aidan Winters?

I pictured him in his penthouse right now, lounging beautifully, probably wearing black silk pajamas. I'd never seen Aidan in black silk pajamas, or any pajamas, but I pictured him wearing them anyway. His dark hair was a little mussed in the picture in my head, his body long and lean and nearly naked. Masculine perfection. A man on top of the world.

He was still waiting for me to text something. So I wrote: *My next condition is that you tell me what you're doing right now.*

He waited a second, and then he wrote: *The truth? I'm walking. It's what I do when I'm at loose ends. I walk the city. I've probably covered every part of it by now. I just spent an hour at the Met and now I'm in Central Park, heading toward Columbus Circle. Not sure where I'll go next.*

I stared at the words in surprise. The man on top of the world was walking alone, probably had been for hours. He did it all the time.

And I realized that the Man in Black wasn't really who he was. It was a costume he put on, a persona. The real Aidan was a runaway kid from Chicago who had come up with an idea with a few of his friends. He might be one of the richest men in New York now, but when he didn't have to be the ice-cold venture capitalist, he was just Aidan, who liked art and wandered the streets of New York with everyone else.

It makes money, but it's utterly cold and unfulfilling, he'd said the night at the art gallery. And the first night we played the game: *I wanted to do this the first second I saw you.* He'd been in character, but he'd been telling the truth. We'd both been telling the truth. It just took playing the game to say what we really meant.

It was time to take a leap of faith. As me.

I lifted my phone again. I texted Aidan my address and the entry code to my building. Then I added the bravest words I'd ever written:

Come over.

THIRTY-ONE

Aidan

FOR A SECOND I stared at Samantha's message as the traffic of Columbus Circle roared past me and New Yorkers bumped into me and cursed me. Then I quickly wrote *Don't change your mind* and got myself a cab.

It took ten painful minutes to get to Hell's Kitchen. I threw money at the driver and got out at Samantha's building. I already knew where she lived, though I wouldn't admit that I'd peeked at her HR file out of curiosity. I wanted to know about the real Samantha Riley, not the roles she played.

I wasn't playing a role myself, not today. I was in jeans and a tee, a baseball cap on my head. I'd just spent an hour looking at Japanese art, because on Saturday morning that was the emptiest part of the Met. The crowds were looking at the Egyptian hieroglyphs and the suits of armor. The Japanese art was some of the most beautiful in the world, and almost no one was there.

I walked to the door of Samantha's building and realized I was nervous. Fucking nervous. I didn't have the suit or the office or any of the other shit I usually had. She'd seen me in jeans and a tee before, but that was when I was playing an airline pilot. *Jesus, Aidan, you're the CEO of a billion-dollar company. Get your shit together.*

I typed in Samantha's entry code. The concierge behind the desk in the lobby gave me a polite nod. When I was dressed like this, I didn't get the extra attention a rich man got and I didn't get kicked out of nice places, like I had when I was a teenager. I was accepted just about everywhere I went without a second glance, except sometimes from women. But I didn't care about any women's opinions right now. I only cared about Samantha's.

I knocked at her apartment and she opened her door. She was wearing black yoga pants and a tee that fell to her hips, her dark blond hair in a ponytail. Her feet were bare. No makeup. She was fucking gorgeous, and all I wanted was to peel those clothes off her and get inside her, make her feel good. Make her feel what I felt. She was so responsive every time I touched her. The air between us was as thick as cream.

She bit her lip, hesitating, and I paused. "Samantha," I said.

"Hi." Her gaze swept down me, slowly, as if she couldn't make herself hurry. Then it moved back up again, and her cheekbones flushed pink. "I, um, I don't usually do this," she said.

I leaned against the doorframe, pressing forward a little so I was edging inside. "Good."

"You know what I mean." She glanced behind her, the line of her neck effortlessly beautiful. "I'm not sure what exactly to do."

"We've done this before," I said.

"I know. But this time, it's you."

Those words hit me: *This time, it's you.* I moved into the apartment and closed the door. I pressed her gently against the closed door and leaned my body into hers, feeling every curve of her. I heard her take a surprised breath.

"You're right," I said. "It's me." I leaned in and kissed her.

She made a sweet, tight sound in her throat and kissed me back, her arms moving around my neck. I opened her mouth and licked slowly into it, and she took my ball cap off and tossed it, her hands running through my hair. Then she tugged at my shirt.

I didn't have to ask her what she wanted—she was telling me. So I pulled my shirt off and tossed it after my hat, then pressed her into the door again. Her thighs went soft against mine and I rubbed my hardening cock against her through my jeans, feeling her legs part. Her hands ran down my shoulders and my back, and she sighed as I kissed her again.

I broke the kiss and explored the corner of her mouth, her jaw, the line of her neck, the tender skin behind her ear. She shivered and I pulled her shirt up, throwing it away and putting my mouth to her neck again. I knew this woman—I knew her familiar skin, the sounds she made when I touched her this way or that. I knew the taste of her and the way she pressed her hips against mine without conscious thought. But at the same time, I wanted to explore her. Our previous encounters had been fraught with tension, the air electric as we tried to figure each other out. Some of them had been achingly fast. Right now, I wanted to explore Samantha. I wanted to know every inch of her, learn what she liked when there were no questions and the clock wasn't ticking. I wanted to know how to please her when it was just her and me.

She liked it when I kissed her neck. I grazed her lightly with my teeth, let my Saturday stubble rasp against her skin, then smoothed it with the tip of my tongue. She shook against me, her fingers curling into me, her breath going short. I touched her nipple through the fabric of her bra, then pulled the strap down and touched the bare skin, brushing over it again and again. She moaned.

She hooked one knee around my hip, and then her other knee over the other, giving me full access to the heat between her legs. I took my cue and lifted her, pinning her to the door, rubbing my cock a little roughly into her through the denim. The friction was harsh and her fingers dug into my shoulders again, this time with her short nails digging into my skin. The sting of it was a pleasant shock and I rubbed into her again, making her hips press back against the door. Even through layers of clothes my cock was aching, the root throbbing, the tip throbbing inside my jeans. I lowered my hands to the perfect curves of her ass and held her up.

I could come like this. Just like this, like a teenager on a second date with the girl he's been after, unable to believe she was kissing him back. Samantha was gripping me, her heels digging into the backs of my thighs as she sighed against me. The combination of soft and bold was intoxicating. I knew by instinct that she had never been like this with other men. She'd never let herself—not until we started the game. She was only like this with me.

"More," she said as I sucked gently on her neck. "Aidan, can we..."

"Yes, we fucking can." I unhooked her knees and slipped her yoga pants and panties off, tossing them away. When I stood again she'd unhooked her bra and dropped it and she stood there perfectly naked. She looked at me, swallowed, and reached for the buttons of my jeans, fumbling with them.

Kicking my shoes off, I helped her. Our fingers tangled. We were definitely like teenagers now, and I realized I was going to be inside her *bare*. The idea made me crazy. Despite how cool I'd played it, I'd never fucked without a condom in my life. This was the right time to do it the first time. She was the right woman.

She was always the right woman.

When we were naked I pressed her against the door again,

skin to skin. I let my hard length drag across her belly as I kissed her again, tasting her soft mouth. I was oversensitized, and every time she moved or breathed I felt it everywhere, like electricity.

Reluctantly, I pulled my mouth from hers. "We can do this however you want," I said. Jesus, we hadn't even made it into the apartment—some romantic I was. "The couch or the bed. Nice and slow or fast and rough. Whatever you want, Samantha."

She reached up and pulled me down so I could smell her skin, damp now with a woman's sweat and the smell of her need. "Aidan," she said, "I feel like I've been waiting forever. Fuck me against the door."

This woman.

I smiled against her skin. "All right, then. Hold on."

THIRTY-TWO

Samantha

FUCK. I'd finally said it. Not *have sex,* or *make love,* but *fuck.* I hadn't just said it, I'd told Aidan to do it. To me. Against a door.

And he'd said yes.

He cupped my ass as I wrapped my legs around his hips. He held me easily and I wrapped my arms around the smooth, hard muscles of his shoulders. He braced me, his long, hard body moving easily, taking my weight. It should have been awkward, but we moved in sync. It should have been unromantic, but it was perfect. We fit together like two pieces of a puzzle. Everything vanished—our real lives, who we were outside this apartment. Our jobs, our pasts. Even the game vanished right now, as I hooked my ankles together and opened to him and he slid into me.

He swallowed my gasp with a kiss. I was drenched, and he was slick inside me, bare. It felt so good. I was familiar with the feel of him, the push of him inside me, but skin to skin was different. I'd never done this with anyone before.

He pushed into me, then moved a little harder, using the resistance of the door behind me and his weight. He was deeper than he'd ever been, and the angle opened me completely. I was pinned, and at the same time I was gripping him, squeezing him, just as active as he was. I hooked my arms around his neck and felt him take me, and at the same time I felt myself take him. Again, and then again, and then again.

"Fuck, Samantha," Aidan said against my neck, his voice rough. "Tell me you feel that."

"Yes." I could barely form even that one small word, my mind was so scrambled, my blood so wild. "Yes."

His arms were like granite, his legs long and strong as he pushed into me, the muscles of his back working as his hips moved. The friction was so intense I felt like the head of a matchstick being rubbed against sandpaper, every touch and movement rasping through my body, the tension unbearable. The way he was angled in me, the way he was moving in me, was making us both crazy, and it was happening fast. I'd always orgasmed fast once Aidan was inside me, but this time was going to set a record. I was going to come.

He said my name again, and then some wild and filthy curse words that made my blood run even hotter. He was as lost as I was. We were both abandoned, up against my apartment door, probably making noises the neighbors could hear. I didn't care. I was about to come, and I was possessive. Everyone could know that this hot, gorgeous man was all mine.

He found my secret, most sensitive spot, the skin behind my ear, and when he dragged his teeth along it, still moving, I came, my nails digging into his skin. As I trembled through it he banged me harder, making the door shake, and then he gasped—the sound was hot and helpless—and came himself. I felt the pulse of it and a warm rush. Then we both stilled, out of breath and panting.

I could feel his sweat against my skin, his heart pounding against mine. I could feel every inch of myself, my whole body humming with pleasure. And I knew that I wanted this, exactly this, as much as I could get it, for as long as I could get it. At any price.

I was in love with Aidan Winters. I also worked for him.

And right now, I didn't even care.

WE DID it right this time. He didn't walk out, and neither did I. We cleaned up, talking a little, the air between us easy. We were still naked, and somehow we ended up in the bedroom, and then we were on my bed. And then we were doing it again, slow and easy this time, Aidan moving above me and then behind me as his hands moved over my skin. I explored him in turn, taking in his shoulders and his chest, the taut lines of his belly and his hips. After the frenzy against my door, we took our time. Aidan was in even less of a hurry than I was, bringing me to the edge of orgasm more than once before finally sending me over.

Afterward we lay lazily in the dim light, talking. He told me about his childhood, his teenage years living with his friends before they formed Tower VC. I talked about my own past, about my parents and my sister, my years working as an executive assistant. That brought us dangerously close to the topic of our working relationship.

Aidan was lying on his back, the sheet pulled carelessly to his waist, one arm crooked behind his head. He looked darkly beautiful, satisfied and relaxed, his hair mussed from sex. "We'll work it out, Samantha," he said, meeting the topic head-on in his Aidan way. "This doesn't have to be an issue at work. I'll make sure of it."

I was lying on my side, watching him. I smiled. "Sleeping with my boss is pretty much the biggest issue there is," I said. "There's no way around it."

He frowned. "We've managed it so far."

We had, but only because of the game. Without the game, it was different. Everything was different. We both knew that.

"My job is important to me," I said.

"I know," Aidan replied.

"And at the same time, I don't want to stop."

"Me neither."

I sighed, tracing my finger along one of his flexed biceps. Now that I had permission to touch him, I couldn't quite stop. "So what's the answer?"

"I have a few ideas. Let me work out the details."

I felt a beat of panic. Everyone knew that sleeping with your boss never worked out—it was practically a Biblical rule. I could hear Emma's disapproving lecture from here. If she found out about this, then I might even be fired from Executive Ranks, sister or not. And if Aidan and I were really going to do this, really going to date, then Emma *would* find out about it. So would everyone at Tower. So would the gossip websites. Which meant my whole life would change.

"What is it?" Aidan said. My hand had stopped moving, and he'd noticed my body tense.

I blinked at him. How serious were we? I hated to be *that girl*, but the stakes were high. Higher for me than for him. If I lost my job, I was unemployed. Aidan would always be the CEO of Tower VC, no matter who he was sleeping with.

Now he had turned his head and was looking at me with concern. "Talk to me, Samantha."

"I just…" I wanted to take the leap of faith. I really did. But

I'd come from nothing, and I'd built my life, and if it fell apart I wasn't sure I could do it again. I didn't even know if Aidan was in this with me if things got hard, or if this was just fun for him and he'd vanish when the difficult questions came up. But we had just had incredible sex—twice—without the game, and now wasn't the time to bring all of this up. We had time to discuss it later. "I'm just not sure it's possible to get the job *and* the guy," I said. "It isn't supposed to be possible."

The lines between Aidan's eyes smoothed, and he smiled at me. His usual cocky self. "Anything's possible if I put my mind to it," he said. "How do you think I got this far?"

THIRTY-THREE

Samantha

AFTER AIDAN LEFT—HE said he had a few things to do tonight—I dozed off. When I woke up, it was late afternoon. I showered, then ate, my body pleasantly hungry. I was also sore in a few spots, which felt good. As I was eating, a text came in from Aidan.

Forgot I promised to attend a benefit tonight. I'll only go for an hour or two.

I wrote back, teasing: *Do you have a date?*

Aidan: *You know I don't. I never do.*

Was that going to change? If we were officially an item, Aidan would take me to social events. I wasn't entirely sure I was ready. Once the gossip sites got wind of me, they'd pick apart my life and my past. I had nothing I was ashamed of, but it was still disconcerting.

And he hadn't asked me to attend with him tonight. He was

right—I wouldn't have gone. This thing, whatever it was, was only a few hours old, and I wasn't ready to face a spotlight. But still, shouldn't he have suggested it? What were we doing?

For a minute, I missed the game, with its rules and its scripts. The game made everything so easy. But no one could play a game forever—sooner or later, you had to be yourself, dealing with the problems of real life.

I tidied my place, washed dishes, laundered my sex-soaked sheets. Just a single girl's quiet Saturday night, while her billion-aire CEO maybe-boyfriend went to a multimillion-dollar benefit. At seven, my phone rang. It was Emma.

"What's wrong?" I asked her when I answered.

"What does that mean?" Emma said.

"It means you're calling me when you're probably working, even though it's Saturday night."

"Tell me the truth," Emma said. "Are you fucking Aidan Winters?"

I nearly dropped the phone. My fingers went numb and my throat closed. Was there a rumor already? "Why would you ask that?" I managed to ask.

"I just assumed," my sister said in her businesslike way. "I know you have the hots for him, and he is extremely bangable. You've been in a relaxed mood lately. I assumed he was getting you off."

My jaw was hanging open. I ignored her crudeness and said, "You guessed? And you were okay with it?"

"It isn't protocol, but I was willing to let it slide. You're both grownups, and like I say, there's the bangable factor. You may be my paragon of a sister, but you're still human."

"I'm not a paragon," I argued.

"Yes, you are. Which is part of the reason I didn't call you on the Aidan thing. I wanted to see you take a chance, do something a little crazy for once. Plus orgasms with a hot guy. So what if he's your boss? It's everything you need in your life."

"Okay, then," I said. "Yes, I'm fucking him. And it's more than that. We're... I think we're a thing."

Emma swore. She had a sailor mouth, foul enough to make me blush. "I'm cutting his balls off," she said when she was finished. "That's it. They're gone."

"Emma, what are you talking about?"

"I'll send it to you," she said. "Then you can look for his remains in the Hudson River." She hung up.

A second later, I got a text. Emma had sent a link, and the simple message: *WTF?*

I clicked the link. It was a gossip site. It had been posted an hour ago. The headline read, "Meet the woman who has finally landed New York's most eligible bachelor!"

Beneath it was a photo of a woman getting out of a black SUV. She was wearing a strapless silver dress over her flawless body. From her looks she was obviously a model. The caption read: "Supermodel Angelica Barnes, who has just broken up with her rocker boyfriend, has found herself a new piece of arm candy for tonight's benefit at the Guggenhiem. You go, Angie!"

Getting out of the car next to her, his hand on her elbow, dressed elegantly all in black, was Aidan.

THIRTY-FOUR

Aidan

SAMANTHA DIDN'T ANSWER my texts on Sunday. She didn't answer my phone calls or messages. She didn't acknowledge me at all.

Something was wrong, but what could I do? Showing up at her building and banging on her door seemed like an asshole move so early in our relationship—our real relationship, that was. If I knew Samantha at all, I knew she wouldn't appreciate a guy who demanded her attention nonstop. Maybe she needed a day of space, especially since we were going to be back to work Monday morning. After a day of impatient fretting, I decided to make sure we talked on Monday.

Except on Monday, she didn't come to work.

"Where is she?" I asked Jade, the receptionist.

"Sick," Jade said. "She called early and said she wouldn't be in."

So her phone wasn't broken, then. It worked well enough for her to call Jade, but not me.

Something was definitely wrong.

I walked back to my office, trying her cell again. No answer. It went straight to voicemail, as if her phone was off.

I had just sat at my desk, perplexed, when Jade rang my desk phone. "I have Emma Riley here, wanting to see you. Were you expecting her?"

I wasn't expecting Samantha's sister, but no way was I going to turn her away. "Send her in."

Emma came in to my office. She was dressed to kill in a pencil skirt and sleeveless top that fit her perfectly. Her red hair was tied up on top of her head.

"Well," she said without preamble, closing my office door behind her and sitting down, "you've done it, Aidan."

"Done what?" I asked.

She rolled her eyes. I'd met Emma once, when I set up the contract for her to find me an executive assistant. Now I could see that she resembled Samantha, though she had a more aggressive air about her. And even without knowing her, I could tell she was definitely pissed at me.

"Of course you don't bother looking at the gossip sites, do you?" she said. "Even when they're talking about you."

She was being rude to a paying client, which meant something was really wrong. "Emma, tell me what you mean."

"That little stunt at the benefit, showing up with a model. You thought she wouldn't see that? I sent it to her myself."

The penny dropped. I pinched the bridge of my nose. That was why Samantha was ignoring my calls. "I gave Angelica a ride because her car service didn't show. We arrived at the benefit and went our separate ways. I don't suppose the gossip sites mentioned that?"

"No. At least, not until today, when Angelica Barnes gave a statement that you two are only acquaintances and are definitely not dating."

"Which I would have told Samantha myself if she'd answered any of my calls or texts. But fine. Once she sees the update, I'll talk to her and explain."

For the first time, Emma fidgeted. "You can't exactly do that."

"Why not?"

"She left."

That made no sense. "Left where?"

"New York."

For a second I was so stunned I could do nothing but stare at her. Then I got up and paced to one end of my office, then the other. "You're telling me," I said finally, "that Samantha—the calmest, most competent person I know—saw a single photo on a gossip site and, without talking to me, she packed a bag and left town?"

"That's what I'm telling you." Emma sighed. "Okay, I agree— it's insane, stupid behavior. And it's nothing like the way she usually acts. In fact, I've never known her to be insane or stupid in my life. That's why this is extra worrying."

I leaned on my desk and looked hard at her. "You know where she is, don't you?"

"She told me, yes, so that I wouldn't worry whether she was safe. But she told me not to tell you, and I promised."

That should have pissed me off. Instead, my mind started ticking, thinking about where she would go. Because there was no way I was going to let Samantha walk out of my life because of one stupid photo. "Why did she do it?" I asked Emma. "She could have called me, even if it was just to yell at me and call me names. Samantha has the coolest head of any woman I've ever met. Why would she pull this stunt now?"

"I think it's for a few days. She'll come to her senses and come back. But she did it in the first place because her pieces are falling apart."

"What the hell does that mean?"

Emma looked thoughtful. "She told you about our adoption, right?"

I nodded.

"It's hard to explain," Emma said. "We have great parents and had a happy childhood. We've both done well. But when you're not only adopted, but abandoned, there's a piece that is always missing. Most adopted kids know there's a record somewhere of who their real parents are, even if they can't access it. Samantha and I don't even have that. We'll live our entire lives without knowing." She looked away, her eyes serious. "And even when you've had a good life like we have, it's like a puzzle piece that's missing. The rest of the puzzle is there, but there's that one hole, and you know you'll never have the piece that fills it. You'll never have the answers." She looked at me. "Her puzzle started breaking apart. It wasn't just that silly photo, Aidan. It was you."

"Me?"

"You've pushed her off balance. She's never had a serious boyfriend in her life, or any man she's had real feelings about. Samantha is like me—everything is under control as long as true emotions aren't involved. Deep feelings mess up your life. Everyone knows that."

I looked at her. Emma might look obviously different from Samantha—the red hair, for one, and she was taller with fewer curves—but when you talked to her, you saw the similarity. Emma was as smooth, as unruffled as Samantha was. She was calm and imperturbable. All the qualities that made for a top-notch executive assistant. She had every detail in place, like Samantha.

At least, until I came along. Now Samantha was a woman who left town on a whim and played hooky from work.

"You're saying she pulled this stunt because she has feelings for me," I said.

"Yes." Now Emma looked annoyed. "What did you do to her? I know my sister. A few dates and nice words from a good-looking man wouldn't do it. Your money would have no effect on her. She's hard to impress—you could put her on your private jet and she would just shrug. Even great sex wouldn't crack Samantha, though I don't want any details, please. So what the hell did you do?"

I dared her to play other roles and be other women, I thought. *I pushed her outside herself and I made all the pieces scramble.* "It's just my charm," I said, deflecting the question. "And I don't have a private jet. I fly commercial. I'm rich, but I'm not an asshole."

Emma still looked annoyed. "Well, if she's just another fuck to you then I'm going to have to castrate you, Aidan. Because you broke my sister."

I raised my eyebrows. I could very easily see this woman robbing a man of his balls and going on with her day. God help any man who tried to take her on—he'd have to have confidence the size of Staten Island.

But if she wanted to do a cold negotiation, then I was her match. Cold was the Man in Black's middle name. "She isn't just a fuck to me," I said. "She's the only woman I want, not that it's any of your concern. And if you think Samantha is broken, then you don't know her as well as you think you do. Are you going to tell me where she is?"

"No," Emma said. "Of course not. That's off the table."

"Then I'd appreciate it if you'd leave, because I'm going to go find her."

She raised her eyebrows. "You think you can do that?"

"I know I can do it within half an hour if I track her credit cards, but I don't need to. I already know where she is."

"You're bluffing," Emma said. "You can't possibly know."

"I already do." I smiled. "Big emotions, Emma. I'm going to go express mine to your sister. You might want to get out of the way."

THIRTY-FIVE

Samantha

PARIS WAS EVEN MORE beautiful than I'd imagined. It was a big city, full of life and intense energy. But the air smelled different than New York, the people were more elegant, and the architecture was some of the most beautiful I'd ever seen.

I stood in the winding neighborhood of Montmartre, looking up at the extravagant, white-domed church of Sacre-Coeur, watching the tourists pass by. I'd just had a baguette with fresh cheese, and in my bag I carried a well-thumbed guidebook and a pamphlet of conversational French phrases. It was all perfect for the role of "American tourist," but this time it wasn't a role. It was just who I was.

How I got here was a blur. There had been that photo of Aidan and my stupid reaction to it. My logical mind had told me that there was a rational explanation, that the Aidan I knew wouldn't spend the morning making love to me while he was already fucking a supermodel. I'd told myself to talk to him about it even as I'd packed my bags and gone to the airport. It was like I was splintered into two people, and the crazy Samantha had already maxed out her credit card on a plane ticket before she even knew what she was doing.

Part of me *wanted* to be run. Part of me wanted any excuse at all.

I'd landed, found a hotel. Remembered to call work and tell them I wasn't coming in. Crashed and slept. Then I'd woken up, showered and changed, and gone walking.

I looked around, letting it sink in for the millionth time. I was really in Paris. I'd gone to the Eiffel Tower first, then the Arc de Triomphe. Being the awestruck American tourist I was. I didn't know where the best bistros or the coolest jazz clubs were. I'd learned the hard way that they didn't do American coffee here, but shots of espresso topped with milk that powered you straight out of your jet lag. I wore jeans and a soft cotton T-shirt and carried a messenger bag. I wasn't sophisticated, and I didn't care. This was the city I'd always dreamed about, the greatest place on Earth.

At the bottom of my bag, my phone was off. Was Aidan still trying to talk to me, I wondered? Maybe he was angry with me by now. I felt an ache deep in my stomach at the thought of him that last day, the way he'd touched me. No man had ever touched me like that, and how it made me feel was terrifying.

I didn't think he would touch another woman like that while he was making promises to me. It was just a photograph. But then again, we'd played a lot of games. Maybe Aidan played other games I didn't know about.

The thought made me want to throw up.

I gazed at Sacre-Coeur for a while, then wandered down the hill to the neighborhood streets. This was idyllic Paris—café's, patios with bright umbrellas, Parisians walking by with their groceries tucked under their arms. I found a café with a menu in English and sat down, ordering a cappuccino.

On the table next to me, left by the last customer, was a copy —an actual newsprint copy—of the *New York Times*. I'd only been gone from New York for just over a day, and still I leaned over and picked it up, leafing through it, the splintered part of me that still longed for New York, and Aidan, eager to scan the news.

My cappuccino came, and I sipped it as I turned the newsprint pages. And then, in the business section, I saw the headline.

The Egerton brothers, the ones who had commented on my ass, were under investigation by the SEC. They'd been set to offer their company publicly on the stock exchange, but then evidence had come to light that proved they had stolen the software that they'd used to launch the company. The theft itself would have gotten them in trouble, but the fact that they were going to sell shares in a company based on fraud brought in federal investigators. The company was finished, there would be no IPO, and both men were looking at criminal charges and possibly jail time.

My mind went back to Aidan at the airport as we'd waited for our flight to Chicago, reading a report about the Egerton brothers on his laptop. *This was originally a revenge thing for me, but now I'm finding interesting information.* And then: *You should know this about me, Samantha. I'm not a nice person, especially in business.*

I had a sinking feeling. Was this Aidan's doing? Because of me?

It was absurd. What kind of ego did I have, thinking that the biggest financial story of the year was because of me? But Aidan had been so sure. And he'd said he had *interesting information.*

I blinked at the story in front of me as the words blurred and came into focus again. If it was true, what kind of person did that make Aidan, the man I'd spent hours in bed with before I left New York? Ruthless. Cold, even. Sure, the Egertons were jerks, and if they'd stolen software and then tried to sell public shares, then they deserved a federal investigation. But now they were ruined, maybe forever. And I had the feeling that Aidan Winters would have no problem sleeping at night.

I closed the paper and pushed it away. Then I reached into my bag and got out my phone. I turned it on, letting it power up and find a signal. Messages and alerts started downloading, several dozen in all. Texts from Emma, who I'd told where I was so she wouldn't worry. And then texts from Aidan.

At first he'd texted me like normal, and then when I hadn't answered he'd been curious. Then alarmed. But the latest text was from an hour ago, and he wasn't alarmed anymore. I scrolled to it and stared at it, taking it in.

I hope you're enjoying Paris, he wrote. *I'm on my way.*

THIRTY-SIX

Aidan

DID she think it was over? She was wrong.

As the plane landed at Charles de Gaulle, I pulled my bag from under my seat. I'd be out of the airport in minutes, because I had no checked bags. Just what I could carry.

I was wearing jeans and a tee. I hadn't shaved and I'd left off the expensive watch. This wasn't a role for me; this was the real Aidan, the runaway kid from Chicago. The woman next to me in the first-class seat had eyed me up and down numerous times, giving me a quiet invitation. The old Aidan would have struck up a conversation with her, given her a fake name, then fucked her anonymously in a hotel somewhere. The new Aidan wasn't interested at all.

I only wanted one woman, and I'd come here to find her.

When I'd come to Samantha's apartment, the game had been over.

But now we were playing again. A new version. And this was the game that I played for forever.

THIRTY-SEVEN

Samantha

I SPENT the next morning in the Louvre, looking at some of the greatest art in the history of the world. It was incredible, but even as I stared at the *Mona Lisa*, I thought of Aidan. I wondered if he'd ever been here and seen this.

I'm on my way, he'd said. But I didn't know what flight he was on or when he'd land. I didn't even know if he was telling the truth. Though something told me that the man who could sink the Egerton brothers with one blow wasn't fooling around.

I walked out of the Louvre, pausing to turn back and look at its astounding beauty. Even with the crowds everywhere, it was breathtaking. I'd kept my phone on, and it sounded in my bag with a text.

Aidan: *Do you want me to guess where you are?*

I didn't even think; that stupid photograph felt like a year ago. I called him.

"Samantha," he said when he answered. "*Bonjour.*"

My knees tried to go weak, right there at the Louvre, at the sound of his voice. I loved his voice. "How did you guess where I am?" I asked.

"It's your happy place, remember? Did you think I wasn't listening?"

My hand was shaking, my throat dry. Just his voice was doing this to me. I'd missed him so much, and it had only been days. I was in big, big trouble.

"You came here for me," I said.

"Yes. I've been here before, though only on business and never as a tourist. I like it. Is it as magical as you thought it would be?"

"Yes," I said, my voice breaking. "Yes, it is."

"I'm glad. I could ask where you are, but you seem to have gone temporarily insane, so you're not going to tell me."

I started walking away from the museum. "I'm not insane." *Just in love with you.* "Just hurt, I think."

"Which means you're insane, because I know you wouldn't believe that I'd leave your bed and go fuck a supermodel. You're far too smart for that."

I hadn't believed it, not really. But he was Aidan Winters, and larger than life. He could have anyone. "It was a moment of weakness," I admitted.

"Her car service canceled on her, if you care. We split a ride, then went our separate ways. But I'm not wasting any more time on that. Right now I'm going to find you."

"How?" I asked, because he had me curious now.

"I could do it nefariously, I admit. I know people who can track your credit card. I know other people who could probably track your cell phone if I paid their fee."

"If you do that, I'll never forgive you."

"I know, and you'd be right. So I haven't done it. Besides, I'd rather guess. It's more fun that way."

I shook my head. "Aidan, Paris is a huge place. There's no way you can guess where I am right now."

"Can't I? You're not at the Eiffel Tower or the Arc de Triomphe, because you've already been there. Those were the first two places you went."

I was silent in shock.

"I'm right," Aidan said with that irresistible cockiness. "I'm trying to figure out where you went next. Montmartre is a Samantha kind of place, but then again so is the Left Bank. I can't decide which one you went to."

Again I was silent, because he was so freaking close. "Are you sure you're not tracking my cell phone?"

"I don't have to," he said. "I pay close attention to you, Samantha. I always have. I think it's Montmartre, because that's where Rachel the art student would go."

I had to pause, because at the mention of that night I felt a rush of pure lust. That night in the rain, going back to his place, stripping, straddling him—everything about it had been hot. I'd come so hard it almost hurt.

"You were fucking magnificent that night," Aidan said, reading my mind. "I've never seen a more beautiful woman in my life."

I made myself speak. "Rachel the art student was a role, Aidan. It wasn't me."

"Your roles were the most honest you've ever been," he said matter-of-factly. "With me, or with yourself. Everything you did while in character told me something about the real you. And I missed none of it."

I had entered a garden now, large and beautifully manicured. The sign said it was called the Jardin de Tuileries. I made a note to look it up in my guidebook. "That still doesn't mean you know where I am," I said. I was starting to enjoy the challenge.

"Leigh the office worker would go to Versailles," Aidan said. "She'd be dazzled by the riches there. Or she'd go to an erotic bookshop to find something to read. Apparently there's one in the suburbs, but the books are all in French. That's sent me back to square one."

He was amazing. I hadn't done either of those things, but given a few more days, I would have done both of them. "Wrong," I said, because I was getting into the game. "I'm not at Versailles. Or at an erotic bookstore."

"One night with the devil, Samantha," Aidan said. "You've already had more than one. Do you want more?"

Yes. I wanted all of it. I wanted everything. "Aidan, I'm your employee. In fact, we're both supposed to be at work right now."

"I told you, I solved that."

"How?"

"Meet me and I'll tell you."

"You haven't guessed where I am yet."

"I will. What's your next objection? Don't tell me it's Angelica Barnes, or any other woman, because we've covered that."

I sat on a bench, ignoring the beautiful gardens around me and the gorgeous Parisians walking by, enjoying it. "I'd be in the public eye," I said.

"You can more than handle it, but if it bothers you, we'll limit our social appearances. That's fine with me anyway. It gives me more time home alone with you in bed."

He was killing me. Killing me. "I'm independent," I said. "I'm used to my space."

"If you want to wait before moving in, then I'll wait."

"I'm not...easy," I said. "I'm messy. Some of my pieces don't fit. I'm still figuring everything out."

"I know. It's what I like about you. I like watching you put your pieces together. It's fascinating. And as an excellent side benefit, the role-playing sex is better than any sex I've even imagined."

I couldn't argue with that. Just hearing him talk about it was making me hot, my skin sensitive under my clothes. It had only been a few days, but it felt like a year since I'd had sex with Aidan.

"Is that what you want?" I asked him. "Sex?"

"With you? All the time, day and night. Was that part not clear?"

Oh, God, that sounded so good. "You know what I mean. Is there more? Because to me, Aidan, there's more. There's a lot more."

"Do you know what I find amusing?" Aidan said. "That you think I flew all the way to Paris to get laid. But if you want to know how I feel, I'll only tell you in person. That's my offer. Your move, Samantha." He hung up.

I put the phone down in my lap, dazed. And turned all the way on. What was I getting myself into? No wonder I'd gotten on a plane to be able to think. Aidan Winters was a lot to handle. Too much for most women.

He isn't too much for me.

I might be figuring myself out, but one thing I had learned was that I wanted a man who wanted everything. A man who pushed me and challenged me and dared me. A man who would fly to Paris for me, just to taunt me when he got here.

I wanted Aidan. He was complicated and brilliant and strangely wonderful. Incredibly sexy. Any woman would get in line for him. I wanted him to be mine.

I picked up my phone again, thinking. We'd talked about Rachel the art student and Leigh the office worker, but we hadn't talked about Sarah the CEO, with her black dress and sexy eyeliner, taking what she wanted from a gorgeous man in a bar.

What would Sarah do?

One night with the devil, Samantha. You've already had more than one. Do you want more?

I swiped my phone awake and sorted through my work email. Sure enough, I found what I wanted—a copy of his travel itinerary with the name of his hotel on it. He might not be able to find me, but as his executive assistant, I could find him.

He was staying at a place called the Parisien, near the Eiffel Tower. I called the hotel. "Good afternoon," I said to the receptionist. "This is Samantha Riley, Aidan Winters' executive assistant. I'll be at the hotel shortly, and I'll need access to his room."

"I am sorry *madame*," the polite Frenchman on the other end of the line said. "We cannot do this without the permission of Mr. Winters, and he is not at the hotel at present. I believe he left an hour ago."

"Then call him and get his permission," I said. "He'll give it. I'll see you in fifteen minutes." I hung up, then stood and walked back toward the street to find a cab.

THIRTY-EIGHT

Samantha

THE PARISIEN HOTEL was beautiful—five stories, built of cream stone, with doors of rich wood reinforced with black iron. Medieval and modern and classic, all in one. I would have looked out of place there in my jeans and tee, but I kept my head held high and my back straight as if I belonged there. It was all in the attitude.

When I told the desk clerk who I was, he slid a key card across the desk to me. "*Merci*, mademoiselle," he said politely. I was almost at the elevator when my phone rang. It was Aidan.

"Coming to my hotel, Samantha?" he said when I answered. "That's a bold move."

My heart was racing, but I tried to sound cool. "What can I tell you?" I said as the elevator doors closed. "You're an excellent salesman. You've almost convinced me, even though you never found me."

"Almost?"

"You said something about talking to me in person," I said. "I'm almost in your room, Aidan. Where are you?"

"Ten minutes," he said, and for the first time he sounded leashed, as if he was keeping control. "I've been out searching for you, but I'll be there in ten minutes. Go in my room and wait for me, and don't take your clothes off."

"I never said I was going to." I was totally going to.

"You can't wait to be naked," he said. "But I'm telling you not to strip. Not because I don't want you naked—I do. I'd just rather take your clothes off of you myself. And believe me, I'll do it slowly just to torture you."

I swiped his keycard and opened the door to his room. "I see. And who takes your clothes off?"

"Eight minutes," Aidan said, and hung up.

He had a luxury room, with a soft sofa and dark wood desk. A bank of windows looked over the 7th Arrondissement. A bedroom opened off to one side. I dropped my messenger bag on the sofa, sat down, and relaxed, toeing off my shoes and flexing my tired tourist feet.

Eight minutes later, the door opened and Aidan walked in. I had to catch my breath. I loved Aidan in a suit, and I definitely loved him naked, but something about Aidan in jeans and a tee made a pulse start deep in my belly, my nipples going raw inside my bra. Our eyes caught, and he ran a hand through his hair, looking me up and down where I lounged on the sofa—fully clothed, as instructed.

"I win," I said.

He shook his head. "Sarah the CEO," he said. "I should have guessed."

I felt myself smiling, a giddy feeling going through my blood. This man just *got* me. Pieces and all, he got me.

He held out his hand, and I took it, standing up. He swung

me over his shoulder as if I was weightless and carried me into the bedroom.

"What are we doing?" I said.

"What I promised," he replied.

He dropped me on the bed on my back and looked down at me. "No shoes," he said cheerfully. "I'll deal with the rest. Slowly."

He undid the button of my jeans and pushed the hem of my shirt up an inch, trailing his fingertips along the skin of my belly. Already I bit back a moan.

"Be quiet," Aidan said. "You're going to be waiting."

He had two days of scruff on his jaw, which was so sexy it drove me crazy. When he tugged my jeans down, his biceps flexed, along with his forearms. "You're in a very good mood for someone with jet lag," I said as the denim slid down my legs.

"I'm going to be inside you shortly, so of course I'm in a good mood," he said.

"You're very sure of yourself."

"Your pants are already off," he pointed out. "Any objections?"

"Not that I can think of."

He slid a hand up my bare calf to the back of my knee, making me shiver. He moved my leg wider and bent to my inner thigh, running his tongue over one spot, then sucking on it, pulling the skin between his teeth. I gasped at the sting, going hot and wet in my panties.

"You taste so fucking good," he said when he finished.

I was breathing hard. "You said you'd tell me what we'll do about our work situation," I managed to remind him.

"Yes, that." He moved to my other inner thigh, positioning my leg just so. He ran a fingertip up almost to my pussy, then down again, watching the goosebumps on my skin. He really didn't seem to be in a hurry. "The company is buying a building in

Chicago," he said. "It's the building the four of us used to live in in the old neighborhood. It's run-down and will be condemned if we don't do something. It isn't our best investment, but the partners don't want to let it go. Call us sentimental, I guess."

I watched as he kicked his shoes off and pulled off his shirt, then got back on the bed between my bare legs. He was impossible to look away from, all dark hair and cheekbones and scruff. "What does that have to do with me?" I asked.

He ran his fingertips along the outside of my hip, over my hipbone, then under my shirt. "It's going to be a special community-building project instead of a for-profit project," he said matter-of-factly. "And you're going to be in charge."

I sat up on my elbows. "Me?"

"Yes, you. You're no longer going to work for me as an executive assistant. Instead you'll work for Tower VC as a special executive, in charge of the Chicago project. What it does, what it costs, everything. The decisions will all be yours."

I stared at him, shocked. He wasn't looking at me—he was inching my shirt up, looking at the skin being revealed on my belly and my ribs. "Aidan, I'm not experienced in that kind of thing."

He shrugged, as if that didn't matter. "You're working with four partners who have experience," he said. "Ask us anything. And since profit doesn't drive this project—real value does—you don't have to be cutthroat. You only have to do what you think is best." He glanced up at me and smiled. "Besides, you can do anything you set your mind to."

His confidence in me made me fall in love with him even further. And it was very, very hot. I met his eye and said, "Do I get a raise?"

He grinned, enjoying this. "We won't discuss money while I'm between your legs," he said, his hand moving up my inner thigh again. "But it will definitely be discussed."

His finger slid into my panties and lightly inside me, rubbing. I gasped and lay back again, luxuriating in the pleasure of that finger. Negotiation or not, with one fingertip Aidan could make me do anything. "I agree," I said.

"Good." His magic fingertip moved to my clit, wetting it with my juices and circling it slowly.

When I was worked up and squirming, he took his hand out again and pushed my T-shirt up, revealing my bra. He took the shirt off, and then the bra, taking his time, touching and kissing my skin. He pulled my panties off, drawing them down my legs. Then he took the rest of his clothes off and positioned himself back between my spread legs, kissing up my inner thigh.

I was going to die of anticipation. I wasn't going to live another ten minutes—I was going to expire. "Aidan," I said, reminding him. "You promised."

He knew what I meant. He skipped over the aching place between my legs, kissing along my hip and sucking at the skin there. "I love you," he said. "Is that what you were waiting for? You didn't have to wait, you know. I would have told you if you hadn't fled halfway across the world."

I ran my hands through his hair as he moved up my body. "I love you, too," I said. "Madly. And you have to admit this way was more interesting."

"It was." He licked my nipple, then moved up to my mouth, which he took—finally—in a deep, long, kiss. When we broke off I was wild for him, open and ready. He slid inside me and we both made a sound of satisfied pleasure.

"You're mine," he said as he started to move. He kissed me again, his stubble scraping my skin as his body owned me. "You're the only woman for me. Admit it, Samantha. You're fucking mine."

"Yes," I said, pulling him down to me, running my lips along his jaw, inhaling him with every breath. "I'm yours. You know all the pieces of me."

He did know my pieces, and he held them with care. He also knew my body, and when I finally came—after long moments of torture—I fell apart.

He came, too, and then he kissed me, a kiss that made me ache and promised me everything. Everything I wanted, everything I was willing to work and sacrifice for. Everything that life could give me. I could have all of it.

As if he read my thoughts, Aidan smiled against my skin. "This is us, Samantha," he said. "This is you and me. Forever."

EPILOGUE

Two years later

Aidan

I IGNORED the jet lag and exhaustion and adjusted my tie in the mirror. I had just come home from a trip to LA, going over entertainment deals with Noah. My plane had landed an hour ago. I'd had time for a quick shower and a change of clothes before I set my evening plans in motion.

The sun had just set, and New York was about to begin its nightlife. Outside the penthouse windows, the city was beginning to light up in its inimitable way. The exhaustion fell away and my blood pumped faster. Tonight was going to be a very, very good night.

I was going to meet a woman tonight.

I wasn't wearing black. Instead I wore charcoal gray dress pants, a pale blue shirt, and a dark blue tie. I took my watch from my side of the dresser—bypassing the jewelry on the other side—and put it on. I put on a spray of cologne, putting the bottle next to the perfume bottle on the dresser.

I walked through the empty penthouse. There was different artwork on the walls now than there used to be, and the sofa now had soft blankets and throw pillows on it. There were framed wedding photos on the mantel. There was tea in the kitchen that I didn't drink and cereal that I didn't eat. Half of my penthouse was no longer mine, and I'd never been happier.

The anticipation built as I got in the elevator, then walked into the lobby. I hadn't seen this particular woman in five whole days—far too long. I hated being away from her for even an hour, but it couldn't be helped. Tower VC was doing better than ever, and the Chicago project was well underway. Both of our schedules were packed. We kept everything straight thanks to Jade, who had been promoted from receptionist to our shared executive assistant.

Besides, these short absences, when we were both out of town, only made the reunion sweeter.

The meeting place we'd picked was a bar a few blocks from the penthouse. It was a high-end martini place, intimate and dark. When I walked in there was a woman sitting at the bar in a black sleeveless linen sheath dress, her hair tied up into a twist at the back of her neck, her long, sexy legs crossed. She wore low heels with ankle straps. As I watched, she took a sip from her martini.

My body went into overdrive at the sight of her. I tried to stay outwardly calm, even though the only thing I wanted to do was take her home, strip her naked, and make her come over and over while I said filthy things in her ear.

She caught sight of me in the mirror behind the bar, and she watched me approach. I wondered what name she'd use. Lately, we used our own names—it was more fun that way.

I slid into the seat next to her. I smelled her scent, glanced at her beautiful mouth and the flawless line of her bare neck. All of her was going to be mine tonight.

Thank God I'd married her a year and a half ago, or I'd be a very filthy man.

She was still looking at me, subtly checking me out in the mirror. I saw her gaze flick to my shoulders, the watch on my wrist. She was just as ready to pick up a stranger as I was. When she put down her empty glass, her diamond wedding ring glinted in the dim light. It had taken me three weeks to pick just the right ring, and she'd never taken it off since the day I gave it to her. I wore my own gold band on my wedding finger.

I ordered my own martini. Samantha's gaze went to my ring as I motioned to the bartender. She licked her bottom lip.

I took my drink and turned to her. She turned to me and smiled.

"I'm Aidan," I said to my wife. "Can I buy you another drink?"

COMING NEXT

Coming in November 2019:
SEXY AS SIN
Dane and Ava's story

Made in the USA
Middletown, DE
01 March 2022

62001868R00137